She'd Wanted To Tell Him.

But she decided there was no point telling him before the child was born, and then decided to wait until Ethan was sleeping through the night so she had a clear head, and then… The longer she left it, the harder it became.

"Pack your bags." Max surged from his chair, strode back to the window. "My son will know me. He'll grow up with his father. I'm seeing to that today."

Gillian gripped the table as though that could anchor her. "I don't understand what you're saying."

"I'm saying," he said quietly, "that we're getting married."

* * *

Don't miss a single book in this series!

The Takeover
*For better, for worse. For business, for pleasure.
These tycoons have vowed to have it all!*

Dear Reader,

I love continuity series—six or so individually terrific books linked so that one teases you for the next, and the next lets you revisit the characters you grew to know and love in the previous one.

This is the first continuity book I've had the pleasure of writing and it's been a fabulous experience working with the authors who've written the other five books. I'm really looking forward to reading all of the stories to see how everything finally plays out.

As for Max and Gillian, whose story this is, it was fun getting to know them. Gillian tried so hard to make the best decisions for the best reasons, even if that reasoning was one Max vehemently disagreed with. And as for Max—a man used to being in absolute control of his life—he never expected a family of his own. Even less did he expect to fall so hard and so completely for Gillian.

Sometimes having our expectations thwarted is the perfect solution.

Enjoy!

Sandra

SANDRA HYATT

REVEALED: HIS SECRET CHILD

Published by Silhouette Books
America's Publisher of Contemporary Romance

Special thanks and acknowledgment to Sandra Hyatt for her contribution to The Takeover miniseries.

To Roberta Brown and Charles Griemsman.
Thank you.

 SILHOUETTE BOOKS

ISBN-13: 978-0-373-73085-8

REVEALED: HIS SECRET CHILD

Visit Silhouette Books at www.eHarlequin.com

Printed in U.S.A.

Books by Sandra Hyatt

Silhouette Desire

Having the Billionaire's Baby #1956
The Magnate's Pregnancy Proposal #1991
His Bride for the Taking #2022
Under the Millionaire's Mistletoe #2056
   "Mistletoe Magic"
Revealed: His Secret Child #2072

SANDRA HYATT

After completing a business degree, traveling and then settling into a career in marketing, Sandra Hyatt was relieved to experience one of life's eureka! moments while on maternity leave—she discovered that writing books, although a lot slower, was just as much fun as reading them.

She knows life doesn't always hand out happy endings and figures that's why books ought to. She loves being along for the journey with her characters as they work around, over and through the obstacles standing in their way.

Sandra has lived in both the U.S. and England and currently lives near the coast in New Zealand with her high school sweetheart and their two children.

You can visit her at www.sandrahyatt.com.

Dear Reader,

Yes, it's true. We're changing our name! After more than twenty-five years of being part of Harlequin Enterprises, Silhouette Books will officially seal the merger by taking the company's name.

So if you notice a few changes on the covers starting April 2011—Silhouette Special Edition becoming Harlequin Special Edition, Silhouette Desire becoming Harlequin Desire, and Silhouette Romantic Suspense becoming Harlequin Romantic Suspense—don't be concerned.

We'll continue to have the same fantastic authors, wonderful stories, eye-catching covers and emotional, compelling reads. We're just going to be moving under the overall company name, which will make us even easier for you to see in the stores, on the internet and wherever you usually find us!

So look for the new logo, but remember, beneath the image will be the same promise of romantic stories of love, passion, adventure, family and a whole lot more. Just the way you like them!

Sincerely,

The Editors at Harlequin Books

One

This time she'd gone too far.

Max Preston looked from the newspaper spread before him to the glittering sea beyond the window and made up his mind. This time he wasn't going to give her the opportunity to ignore his calls. To ignore *him*.

His chair scraped across the parquet flooring of the Beach and Tennis Club's breakfast restaurant as he stood from his table. Leaving a tip for his waitress and his just delivered omelet untouched, he took one last sip of his coffee and left.

So much for the first Saturday off he'd had in months.

He hadn't known he was going to fill his morning. He did now.

A search on his phone as he strode to his car turned up her address. Tossing the parochial, two-bit rag she worked for—the proverbial thorn in his side—onto the passenger seat, he slid into his seat and eased the Maserati out of the club's parking lot.

The first time he'd seen Gillian Mitchell's picture and
byline in the *Seaside Gazette* and realized that she was here
in Vista del Mar, he'd felt an unexpected surge of pleasure
and triumph, like when he found something he didn't realize
he'd lost and was missing. A hundred-dollar bill in his coat
pocket—but better.

It only took the seconds he'd needed to read her first biting
paragraph for those feelings to vaporize.

Since that moment, he'd been trying to view her presence
here and her articles with purely professional detachment.

Clearly, she wasn't doing the same. Her attacks on Cameron
Enterprises and, in particular, Max's boss, Rafe Cameron,
might, to the uninformed reader, appear objective, but they
were personal and directed at Max. He was sure of it.

On the seat beside him, her opinion piece lay face-up. At
the first set of lights he flipped the paper over so that he
didn't have to see the one-sided article that constituted her
opinion.

A call came through on his cell. "Max speaking," he said
into his earpiece.

"Have you seen it?" Rafe wasted no words.

"I'm dealing with it." As head of PR for Cameron
Enterprises it was Max's job to smooth the waters, to make
sure the people of Vista Del Mar saw Rafe's takeover of Worth
Industries—a microchip manufacturer and one of the town's
biggest employers—in the best possible light.

And Gillian, it seemed, was doing everything in her power
to achieve the opposite result.

"Is it libel?" Rafe asked.

"It's close. I'm on my way to see her now. I'll let her know
how seriously we're taking this. That our lawyers will be
examining this piece as well as every word she's written to
date, and every word she will write in the future on anything
related to this subject."

"Good." Rafe rang off.

At one time, Max had nothing but the highest respect for Gillian's doggedness. But when she started making his boss the repeated target of her campaign, that doggedness looked a lot more like intransigence and plain old sour grapes.

Because she and Max had history.

But the way he remembered it, it had been good history. And it had ended cleanly. Six months into their relationship, when she'd casually dropped the words *children* and *marriage* into a conversation, he'd known he had to end it. It was only fair. He didn't do marriage and kids, they hadn't been in his plans. Still weren't. And till that moment he hadn't thought they'd been in hers.

So he'd broken it off with her. On the spot. It was the only honest thing to do. And he'd thought she'd taken it well. There had been no drama. She'd calmly agreed with him that they clearly had different needs from a relationship, and walked away without so much as a backward glance.

He hadn't heard from her or of her in the three and a half years since then. Till these opinion pieces and her supposed factual, objective articles. So now he was thinking maybe she hadn't taken it well. Maybe she had merely bided her time till the opportunity to strike back arose.

The ten-minute coastal drive gave Max time to calm down so that by the time he reached her place—an older Spanish-style home set several blocks back from the beach—he was only annoyed instead of furious.

She was nothing he couldn't deal with.

And, if he was honest, he was just a little curious, too. They'd had some good times. Had she changed in the intervening years? Were her eyes as green as he remembered?

He strode the path to her door, knocked firmly and waited, standing where she'd have a clear view of him through the glass bordering the door. He could just make out the beat of the rock music she used to enjoy and had a flash of memory, of Gillian swaying and sashaying around her L.A. apartment. The music stopped.

Beyond a row of orange flowering bushes, a blue hatchback with tinted windows sat in the driveway. Max paused before knocking again. She used to drive a sporty, two-door soft top.

Had she married, as she'd been so clearly keen to do? The thought gave him pause. The fact that she hadn't changed her name didn't mean she hadn't gotten her wish. The hatchback had a definite family-car aura to it.

It didn't matter. The only thing that concerned him was the paper he held and the inflammatory words she was writing in it. As he lifted his hand to knock again, the door swung open halfway.

For a moment, as they looked at each other, the world stopped. For just that moment, he forgot why he was here. Sunlight caught her chestnut-brown hair, brought a luminescence to her creamy skin. She was so hauntingly familiar, and yet, not.

"Max?" She blinked, regrouped. "What are you doing here?" Her words, the shock and the underlying reluctance in them, got the world spinning nicely again. He hadn't expected or wanted warmth, but he also hadn't expected fear, and that was definitely what he saw in her wide, green eyes and heard in the catch in her throaty voice. She didn't want him here.

"We need to talk."

"If you want to talk to me, phone." She swung the door.

Max put his hand and foot out to halt its momentum. "You'll see me now. I tried phoning last week, remember? That didn't work. This is what you get when you don't answer my calls."

"I was going to call you Monday. We can make an appointment. I'll see you during normal working hours."

Her eyes were just as green as he remembered. It was the emotion he read in them now that was different. Perhaps the defensiveness was caused by conscience about the things she was writing. "And since when have you kept normal working hours?"

"Since…" A look he couldn't interpret stole over her face. "Since I realized that work isn't the be-all and end-all of everything. Which means that, unlike yours, my weekends are sacred. I like to relax, to devote my time to…other things. It most definitely means that you're not a welcome intrusion."

Max stayed precisely where he was. He remembered her as being direct but beneath this morning's directness he couldn't help but feel that she was hedging. She was on the defensive. Which worked for him. "You're not the only one who values their weekends," he said, "so let me come in, we'll talk, straighten a few things out and then I'll leave. But until we've talked, I'm not going anywhere."

Gillian glanced at the slim watch encircling her wrist then over her shoulder as though deciding. "Five minutes, Max. That's all I can give you." She stepped back from the door, opened it just wide enough for him to enter.

It was a decision that pleased him. "Five minutes is all we'll need. So long as you see reason." He stepped inside, got his first proper look at her. A white tank top clung gently to the curve of her breasts. The press of her nipples against the soft fabric advertised the fact that she wore no bra, diminishing the available oxygen in the room and threatening to distract him absolutely. For the first time Max reconsidered the wisdom of catching her unawares, first thing in the morning, in her home.

Drawstring yoga pants rode low on the flare of her hips. Her pale feet were bare. He was guessing she wasn't long out of bed. And he was *not* going to follow that train of thought any further, because combining the words *Gillian* and *bed* even if only in his mind would almost certainly derail his thought process.

Though still slender, she was maybe a little curvier than he remembered. There was a new softness to her body that was most definitely missing from the guarded expression on her face.

She bit her lip, something he'd only ever seen her do when she was nervous, then gestured to a room just off the entranceway. She stood blocking any view he might have had of any of the rest of her house while he stepped into the formal living room she'd indicated. How did she manage to look so unyielding and yet so tempting?

A sofa and two comfortable-looking floral armchairs surrounded a coffee table that was bare except for a flowering peace lily. The curtained window overlooked a private, palm-filled garden.

"Sit down." She pointed to one of the armchairs. "I'll be back in a moment." She headed for the door.

"One thing."

She hesitated.

"Are you married?" He hadn't meant that to be the first question he asked her.

"No."

He shouldn't feel relief, he had no right, and he was no hypocrite. Not normally. Business. This was purely business. That was all there would ever be between them.

She left the room and Max had to drag his gaze from the sway of her hips in the soft draping fabric and turn back to the living room. The door shut with a firm click behind her.

He looked about the room that seemed both a little old-fashioned and far too tidy, in an almost sterile way. The Gillian he remembered used to have half-read newspapers, magazines and books stacked and stashed around any and all of her living spaces.

Seemed she'd changed. Or that this was what his grand-mother used to refer to as her company room. It certainly wasn't where the music he'd heard or the scent of coffee he'd caught as he'd stepped into the house had been coming from.

He placed his copy of the *Seaside Gazette* on the coffee table so that her opinion piece was uppermost, reminding him to refocus on his sole reason for being here. Not to speculate on Gillian's life.

True to her word she was back in just a few moments, once again shutting the door carefully behind her. The soft tank top and yoga pants had been replaced by hip-hugging, multipocketed cargo pants and an olive-green T-shirt. Thank-fully, for the sake of his focus, it seemed she wore a bra beneath the T-shirt. She'd pulled her lush hair back into a high ponytail.

She looked like the heroine from one of the computer games they used to play—ready for combat.

The subtle charge of anticipation swept through him. "This morning's opinion piece." That was why he was here. Not to find out if she was married or how she'd been doing in the past three and half years, or...if she wanted to go out to dinner tonight. There was, after all, more than one way to skin a cat.

No. Not going there again. Max pulled himself up short.

Her kick-ass demeanor had beguiled and fooled him once into thinking it meant she didn't want those things he shied away from, that she wasn't looking for emotional intimacy and a future together. And Max was a man who learned from his mistakes.

Gillian perched on the edge of the second armchair, as though ready to leap back to her feet. Her expression was shuttered. Still, just because they were on opposite sides of this issue didn't mean he couldn't enjoy locking horns with her. "It's libelous," he said quietly, leaning toward her.

"No, it's not." She shook her head, smiling. "It's an opinion piece. And every opinion is backed up by cold, hard facts."

"You call labeling Rafe Cameron an angry teenager who's grown into an angry man with an ax to grind and the money to grind it well, a fact?"

"*I* didn't call him that. It's a direct quote."

"From a real person?"

"Of course." He'd pushed a button with that one. "As real as Emma Worth was."

And she pushed a button right back. Max's jaw tightened. Emma Worth's father, Ronald, had founded Worth Industries and was revered in the town. So when Gillian had quoted his skeptical daughter in a piece two months ago, the townsfolk had sat up and taken notice. And not in a good way. In the interim, Max had brought the focus back round to the good work Rafe was doing in the town, specifically the charity, Hannah's Hope, he'd founded to improve the literacy skills of the town's workforce, many of whom were migrant workers with limited formal education.

He had scored something of a coup in using Rafe and his half-brother Chase's connections to secure the involvement of superstar musician Ward Miller. The community was justifiably enthusiastic, almost excited. And interest in the upcoming fundraising gala was strong and building. Negotiations with a number of other celebrities were proceeding nicely.

But celebrities were notoriously sensitive about their public images. They were rightly cautious about what and whom they were linked with.

Gillian and her opinion pieces could end up scaring some of his best prospects off for no good reason. "You at least gave Emma a name. I had no doubt she was real. Today's source…" He shrugged to express his doubts.

"Emma insisted I use her name because she knew it would give weight and credence to her comments. The source I used for today's piece didn't feel the same way. And I agreed with him. But that doesn't mean he's not real or that he didn't have specific, verified examples to back his opinion up."

Max leaned back in his chair and studied her, trying to gauge just how sure of her position she was. "You're skating on wafer-thin ice, Gillian. Our lawyers will be taking a good hard look at each and every word you've written."

"They can look as hard as they want." Defiance lifted her chin. And he found he was the one doing all the "looking." Her hair, her skin, her figure, the fire in her green eyes that picked out flecks of amber. He cataloged her features, remembered how he'd liked so much—everything, in fact—about her, but it had been her eyes, the intelligence and passion they hinted at, that captured his attention most.

He wouldn't be distracted by the battle light in them now, although he could admit it stirred reactions in him that he'd had no intention of allowing. But there was no denying she was beautiful, all the more so when the passion for one of her causes was stirred.

Once, he'd had no trouble making passion, of an altogether different kind, stir.

He'd never met anyone quite like her, either before or after their time together. And he so didn't need to be going down that track now. He tapped his fist on the newspaper. That was why he was here. "You're unnecessarily inciting uncertainty, fear and anger. Cameron Enterprises is putting a lot of resources into Hannah's Hope and the upcoming gala, with the aim of giving something back to the community. The charity can do a lot of good for the town, but not if you scare people off it." He deliberately didn't try to tell her his boss's takeover of Worth Industries would ultimately be good for the community. Or that Rafe was behind the charity for any reason other than to improve the public image and perception of his business till his plans for the future of the business were finalized.

Rafe could still jump either way with those plans.

"I'd say it *is* necessary to give voice to the opinions in that piece," she said. "The citizens of Vista del Mar ought to be uncertain. They ought to be angry and afraid. They ought not to trust in the goodness of Rafe Cameron's heart."

"Seems to me you're letting personal animosity impact professional integrity." Even if she was right.

For a second, her jaw dropped. "There's nothing personal about this."

"You're not using this as an opportunity to get back at me?"

Her laughter was short but the amusement real. "You flatter yourself, Max."

"Do I?"

"Yes. I call it as I see it. If I suggest some questions that the people of Vista del Mar might like to ask your Mr. Cameron then that's just doing my job, regardless of who he employs as his spin doctor."

"And if our lawyers have some questions they want to ask you and the paper's owners, they'll just be doing their job."

"I have the complete backing of the paper's owners."

"Nobody likes to be sued," he said quietly. "It'll be easy enough to call them off. All you have to do is to stop writing such aggressively provocative pieces. Stick to the truth and the facts."

She tilted her head, frowning. "Are you threatening me?"

"No. I'm just letting you know what you're getting into. Giving you the facts."

She shook her head slowly. "Have you forgotten that much about me, Max? Do you really think threatening me, because that was a threat, not a helpful passing on of information, is going to make me shirk my duties as a voice in this community?"

"I am trying to help you. You need to know how things stand. Rafe Cameron doesn't let people get in the way of what he wants and he doesn't mess around." He hoped, for her sake, that she believed him.

"Can I quote you on that?"

"No. This is a visit between old…friends." Any other word was too loaded. "I can, however, get you quotes on and from Rafe himself. An interview if you'd like."

A smile spread across her face. It seemed, in fact, to brighten the whole room. "Do you mean like the type of information you'll be putting across at your upcoming press conference, or the whitewashed press releases out of your office? Like that one that came across my desk last week full of glowing praise for Hannah's Hope and the gala?"

That was precisely what he'd been thinking of. Only he could hardly admit that now.

"As if it wasn't obvious from the—" A sound—something soft hitting the floor upstairs—stopped her midsentence and wiped all trace of amusement from her face. She glanced at her watch. "Your time's up, Max. I've heard you out. I'll think about what you said. Really, I will." She was suddenly reasonable, her tone conciliatory. "I promise." She stood and walked to the door, opening it. "Just go."

Max rose slowly. Something had thrown her off her stride, put that fear back into the eyes that were now fixed on him as she waited for him to move. *Willed him to move?* Watching her, he walked toward her. She turned and headed out of the room. By the time he caught up to her she was standing at the front door, holding it wide to reveal the morning sunshine.

He paused.

She opened the door wider still.

"It doesn't have to be like this, Gillian."

"Yes it does." Her words were clipped. "I do my job as I see fit."

"I wasn't talking about your job. I was speaking... personally. We were rivals once and still managed—"

"I learned my lesson and now I keep my personal and my professional lives separate. So, please, just go. Now." She reached for him, her fingers closing around his arm, as though to urge him through the doorway.

Max stayed where he was, her desperation making him curious. Something wasn't right here. Did she have a man back there, someone she didn't want him to see?

Another soft thump and he looked deeper into the house to where it had come from.

"Max," she hissed his name and tugged his arm. "Not now." Panic tightened her voice.

Max gave it up and took a step. He wasn't going to care. Either about what she was trying to hide or about unsettling her by lingering or about how that simple touch, her hand on his arm, had resonated through him.

"Mommy," a happy singsong voice called. She let go of his arm and her hand fell to her side.

"Mommy?" he asked, unable to keep the shock from his voice. She closed her eyes and her shoulders sagged. The pieces dropped into place—the hatchback, her softer curves, her haste to get rid of him—it suddenly made sense. She might not be married but she certainly hadn't wasted any time in replacing him in her bed, in finding someone to give her the child she'd talked about. "When did that happen?" Max was no expert on children, he had no idea how old the child might be. Anywhere less than three but old enough to talk. So, not a baby.

"Go. Please," she repeated, but this time the authority had

gone from her command. A bleak resignation filled her eyes. "I need to talk to you. But not now. Not here."

"Sure." Definitely time to go if there was a child here. He barely knew how to be in the room with his own nieces. And he was still processing the fact that Gillian had had a child.

"Mommy."

One glance. That was all he'd allow himself to satisfy his curiosity. Max turned back to see a little, curly-headed boy, clutching a faded blue blanket, standing at the foot of the stairs.

"I'm hungwy."

A little boy, who was the spitting image of Max and his brother in the picture his parents still had on their hallway wall, taken when he was two.

Shock swamped him. He, not Gillian, was the one who'd been skating on thin ice. And he'd just fallen through into a paralyzing new world.

Max looked from the boy to Gillian. Her skin, always pale, had faded to ashen, her knuckles as she gripped the door handle were white.

"Mommy?" He echoed the child's word, not taking his eyes from her. "Mommy?" And for a second he wished that he, too, had the door handle to hold on to, to steady himself. The boy was Gillian's. The boy who looked like Max. He didn't need to do the math to know the child was his.

"Okay, honey," Gillian said, her voice soft, "go on into the kitchen. I'll come get you some cereal." The boy looked steadily at her and Max for the longest time then trotted through a doorway.

The depth of her deceit stunned him.

And to think he'd attributed her defensiveness to conscience over the piece she'd written. That wrong didn't even register on the same scale as the deception she'd practiced on him for the past three and a half years.

"I don't suppose we can talk about this later?" Her eyes didn't quite meet his, and her throat moved as she swallowed. She knew there was no way he was leaving now.

He took hold of the door and swung it shut.

The fury was back in full force as he followed her to the kitchen. Overlaying a deep and utter shock. Shock that he couldn't process and fury that he couldn't give vent to now, not with a child here.

A boy.

His son.

TWO

Gillian's stomach churned. What was going to happen now? She knew only one thing. She knew it the instant Max recognized himself in Ethan.

The carefully protected bubble of her life was about to be blown apart. She followed Ethan through to the kitchen. Every slow deliberate step of Max's Italian-loafer-clad feet sounded like an ax fall behind her.

But underneath her anxiety she recognized a flicker of relief. The relief a condemned man might feel on his way to execution. If nothing else, the agony of anticipating the inevitable was over.

She'd known Max was head of PR for Cameron Enterprises. She'd known, therefore, that her articles had the potential to bring her into contact with him. And that perhaps the time had come to tell him about Ethan.

But not in her own home. She'd never thought that. Not where he could see her son. Not without her first doing the impossible and preparing Max for the news.

In the center of the kitchen she stopped as Ethan climbed onto his booster seat at the table. So much about her kitchen and its cozy dining area advertised the fact that a child lived here. Which was why she hadn't brought Max to this room in the first place.

Her half-drunk coffee sat on the opposite side of the table from Ethan. The same newspaper that had brought Max to her door lay folded to reveal the crossword, reminding her that a mere ten minutes ago her biggest problem had been finding an eleven-letter word for *incident*.

Her day had stretched out, relaxed and pleasant, before her.

She needed to move, to be doing something. Keeping her back to Max and Ethan, she poured a bowl of cereal. With hands that weren't quite steady, she sliced banana into the bowl and added milk, but there was only so long she could drag the preparation out. Eventually, she had to turn from the counter and face the music. Or in this case the absolute silence.

Max sat in the chair she'd vacated earlier, opposite Ethan. They were staring at each other—from perfectly matched blue eyes—with unabashed curiosity. Ethan could outstare almost anyone. She now realized where that ability had come from.

Gillian set her son's bowl in front of him, milk slopping over the side as she did so. Her hands clenched into fists, her nails dug into her palms. She had to calm down, take control, of herself and of the situation.

Ethan, having looked his fill at the stranger, picked up his spoon and began eating, his breakfast now more important than the man at the table. Gillian found a cloth for the spilled milk.

And Max…watched.

He still hadn't spoken a word and his silence may not be

affecting Ethan, but every second of it ratcheted up the tension in her stomach. "Do you want coffee?"

He shook his head. A single abrupt movement.

She'd known her son looked like his father, but seeing them here together for the first time, the resemblance was even stronger than she'd realized. Seeing them here together was both her greatest wish and her greatest fear.

"What's your name?" Ethan had stopped spooning cereal into his mouth long enough to ask the innocent question.

Max opened his mouth.

"His name's Mr. Preston," she said before Max could supply anything confusing or startling, because she'd suddenly had the terrifying thought that this man, who'd had no intention of ever being a father, had been about to say "Daddy."

"Pweston."

"We'll find something else for you to call me," Max said, the piercing blue of his arctic gaze firmly on Gillian. He looked back at her son. "What's your name?"

"Ethan. An' I'm gonna be three soon. How old are you?"

Max's eyebrows shot up. Clearly he wasn't used to the directness of a child's questioning. He ought to be, he was pretty good at it himself. A smile lifted the corners of his lips, momentarily smoothing the deep lines that had furrowed his brow. "I'm thirty-two. Nearly thirty-three." His gaze swung to her. "Which means I was thirty when you were born."

Not here. Not now. Gillian tried to telegraph the silent message to him. Not in front of Ethan. "His birthday is the same day as yours," she said quietly. Max jerked back as though she'd hit him.

"Do you wanna see my twain?"

"Yeah," he said, to all outward appearances calm and back in control, "I'd like that."

Max stood and father and son left the table, Ethan trotting ahead, Max tossing aside his leather jacket and modifying his stride to follow. Gillian couldn't bear to follow but knew she had to. She had to be there in case Max said anything to upset or confuse Ethan.

As calmly and as quietly as he'd sat at the table, she could tell he was livid. But that anger was for her. She didn't think he'd let Ethan see it—after all, he was better than any man she'd ever met at controlling his emotions.

With dragging footsteps, she followed. She stood in the doorway and watched as, for twenty minutes, Max lay on his side, propped up on one elbow on her family room floor, his long legs stretched out and his shirtsleeves rolled up, playing trains with his son. The sight was as surreal as if James Bond had waltzed in and done the same thing. With an obedience that had to be alien to him, he pushed engines and carriages around a blue plastic track, taking garbled advice from the expert on the trains' names and what they carried and the appropriate noises to make. The two of them spun stories and orchestrated derailments.

It broke her heart.

She thought she'd done the right thing.

She was so *sure* she'd done the right thing. For everyone. For Max because he didn't want a family, for Ethan because he deserved better than a father who didn't want him and for her because she hadn't wanted to trap, or be trapped with, a man who didn't love her, who didn't open up emotionally, who would always put his career ahead of anything else in his life. Who would ultimately, in the ways that counted, reject her and their son.

She'd thought she could provide all that Ethan needed.

But now? A chasm had opened and uncertainty flooded in.

For the first time since they'd come into the room, Max looked at her. The light, the softness, the pleasure that had been in his eyes, dimmed and hardened. In one swift movement he stood. "Are you all right here, son, if I go and talk to *Mommy?*"

"Son"? Gillian went cold. It was just an expression. He wasn't the first man to call Ethan "son." It didn't mean anything. Despite the fact that he was the first man for whom it was truly more than just an expression.

Ethan didn't look up from the train he was pushing toward a tunnel as he said, "Uh-huh." She hadn't had any daddy questions from him yet. She'd known they'd come one day but she'd hoped that day was a long way off.

A tendril of fear snaked through her. What if there was more to Max's reaction than anger over the secret she'd kept? What if he wanted to claim Ethan? Max, because of his nature and his profession, chose words carefully. And if he'd called Ethan "son"...

He wouldn't. He couldn't.

Two long strides had Max at her side, his fingers gripping her elbow as he spun her and led her back to the kitchen. Three years and he still used the same cologne. Eternity. The one that made her think of him whenever she'd smelled it. The scent reassured her. He was a creature of habit. He didn't change his ways for anyone. He wouldn't want a son. There would be no room in his life.

Her legs unsteady, and needing some kind of barrier in front of her, she sat at the table. She traced a scar in the old wood with her fingernail as he paced her too-small kitchen, tension and anger radiating off him in waves.

He'd always been passionate—about his career, his life and at one point about her. She could still vividly remember their lovemaking. But now that passion was channeled into anger. The fact that he hadn't yet given vent to it gave her a clue as to how powerful it was.

If he decided he wanted visitation rights she'd give him that, but only if he could guarantee that it would be permanent, that… Gillian threaded her fingers into her hair. Where was she going with this?

He was still pacing and turning. Gillian kept her gaze on the table but she heard his step, felt his presence surrounding, suffocating her. If only he'd say something. Anything. Finally, the footsteps stopped.

"He's my son."

Anything except that.

The controlled, quietly spoken words, that simple statement of fact, contained a wealth of emotion. But they hadn't been a question so Gillian said nothing.

"How dare you?"

That, however, was most definitely a question. She looked up. He stood with his back to her looking out the window above the counter and she was grateful she didn't have to meet his gaze. "I did what I thought was best."

He spun back to her. "Best?" He ground the word out, ice in his gaze.

She had to force herself to meet that anger, feel that wintry animosity. "You didn't want children. You broke up with me because I mentioned the word just once."

He shook his head in disbelief. "You were pregnant then?"

"Yes."

"How?"

"Do you remember that week we both caught a stomach virus?"

"The one I picked up on a trip to Boston and passed to you?"

"I didn't think I'd been that sick." She lifted her shoulder. "But it interfered with the pill and I got pregnant."

"And you didn't—" He turned back to the window. "I'm that boy's—"

"Ethan's."

He crossed to the table, leaned on his fists, his face close to hers. Her heart thundered but she wouldn't back away from his intimidation.

"I'm Ethan's father." His voice was lethally calm, but a bluish vein pulsed in his temple. "And you never once thought I had a right to know that."

She'd thought it a million times but common sense had always prevailed.

"Are you my daddy?"

Gillian's heart plummeted at her son's happy, singsong question. Inquisitive and bright with the hearing of a bat, he never missed a thing.

For an instant, Max's gaze fixed on hers and for the first time there was something other than anger in it. Was he looking for her permission? She shook her head. "No," she whispered. "Not now."

His gaze hardened. "If not now, then when?" Max pulled out the chair next to Gillian, spun it so it faced Ethan, and sat leaning his forearms on his knees, putting himself closer to Ethan's level. "Yes. I'm your daddy," he said gently.

So much for needing her permission.

She watched her son for his reaction. Ethan frowned, stared at Max for a few seconds, and then smiled. "Come play."

Max glanced questioningly at Gillian. If he'd expected Ethan to be as stunned by the discovery as he'd been, he was very much mistaken.

She stood. "How about I put your favorite movie on, honey?" Normally, Gillian discouraged the watching of TV. Today was not normal. "The one about trains."

"Okay." Ethan headed blithely for the family room.

When she got back, Max was exactly where she'd left him, sitting in the chair, staring at the doorway, forearms resting on splayed knees. "Did you have to tell him that?"

He jerked upright. "I was hardly going to leave it to

you," he said quietly. "He deserves to know before he turns eighteen."

"He's never asked."

"Well, he did and now he knows. And at least now he doesn't have to call me Pweston." And for just a second a wry smile lifted a corner of his lips and amusement passed between them. Then vanished. "I had a right to know, too, before he came looking for me wanting to know why he'd grown up without his father."

"You didn't want children."

"I didn't want to do jury service last year, either, but I did, and I coped and I think I did a good job."

"Ethan deserves better than a father who's only there because he has to be."

"It's better than no father at all."

"Is it? I didn't think so." She'd had a reluctant, resentful, part-time father for her early years. It had taken her many more years to realize that his attitude and actions and eventual desertion were not a reflection of her worth. Even so, his rejection of her had shaped who she was.

"Clearly. But family is important. Having a mother and a father, that's how it's supposed to be."

"Only if that mother and father both want to be there. Only if neither of them is resenting the child for its very existence."

His gaze was cold on her face till finally, after a silence that stretched and hardened like a wall between them, he spoke.

"I had a right to know, and you denied me that right. You denied me two years and ten months of my child's life?"

Gillian said nothing. She'd made the best decision she could with the facts she had at the time. And the fact was that Max had wanted nothing permanent in his life. Not a relationship and certainly not a child. For all the grueling and lonely time over those years, they had also been the best, most satisfying times of her life. She'd seen her son grow from a baby, his personality developing. It had been a privilege and a delight and she'd denied Max that opportunity. High-flying, career-driven, workaholic Max Preston who wouldn't have time in his life for a child. Who'd said he didn't want children. Ever.

High-flying, career-driven, workaholic Max Preston who'd just spent half an hour on her family-room floor playing trains. She wanted to weep. "If you'd called just once, just once, after we broke up…"

He shook his head. "Don't you dare try to blame me."

"I'm not. I'm just…" She didn't know what she was. Confused? Anxious?

Max surged from his chair, strode back to the window.

"This changes everything." He turned back to her. "Pack your bags."

"What do you mean?"

"I mean pack your bags. My son will know me. He'll grow up with his father as part of a family. I'm seeing to that today."

Gillian gripped the table as though that could anchor her. "I don't understand what you're saying."

"I'm saying," he said quietly, "that we're getting married."

Three

Married?

Surely she had misheard him.

She'd never been good at reading his face but there was no mistaking the implacable seriousness of his voice.

And it terrified her.

But now was not the time to give in to, or even show, her fear. She thought frantically. This Max was not the man she'd thought she knew. "Maybe I owe you something." Gillian spoke calmly, surprising herself with her composure. Deliberately, she released her grip on the table and rested her hands in her lap.

Where they clenched into fists as she struggled to find her center in a world that was spinning, threatening to spiral out of control.

"Damn right you do."

"And yes, maybe we need to work something out but—"

"There are no maybes and buts, and there's no *we*. I've already worked it out."

She remembered that about him, how decisively he acted. She used to like that confidence, that absolute certainty, but what she needed from him now was compromise and recognition that there would have to be negotiation. So it was up to her to be the reasonable one.

He'd see sense.

He had to.

She stood and crossed to him. The cold fury he radiated stopped her from getting too close. But she knew there was a reasonable man inside there. Once he'd let her see glimpses of a loving side that had enamored her. "You can see Ethan as much as you want. You can have visitation on the weekends, I won't argue with that. Of course, initially, I'll have to be there at all times, to reassure him, but as he gets used to you—"

"You have no idea, do you?" Max closed what remained of the gap she'd left between them, drawing himself up to his full six feet, using every tactic, and none of them subtle, to dominate. "I've already missed out on two years and ten months of my son's life." He spoke quietly. "I'm not settling for visitation on your terms on the weekends. But I can be reasonable."

Gillian dared to hope.

"I'll give you two options. You come to Vegas with me right now and marry me—giving Ethan a father who is married to his mother." His gaze raked over her. Such coldness where once there'd been such heat. Once just a look between them and passion combusted. "And don't worry," he said as though he'd read her thoughts, "I won't be claiming any marital rights. Anything I felt for you is long dead."

Gillian held herself utterly still, showed no reaction. If he was lashing out now, it was no more than she expected. All she needed from him was a glimmer of reasonableness. "And my second option?" She held tight to her faint hope.

Ethan's gurgling laughter drifted through from the living room. Max glanced that way before training his hardened gaze back on her. "Or we face off in court. And it'll be you who's fighting to get weekend visitation rights."

That faint hope withered. "You wouldn't." But she didn't believe her own assertion. "You wouldn't take him from me."

"Just try me, Gillian. You had no qualms about taking him from me."

Cold dread seized her. He would do it. He was ruthless enough and furious enough. And rich enough.

She had her salary from the newspaper, and she could sell this house she'd inherited from her grandmother, and she even had a small nest egg—for a rainy day. It was no insurance against the storm of the century that Max could call down on her shoulders. He'd use the Preston millions to fight for custody of her son. Make sure he got his way. She wouldn't stand a chance.

He slid his phone from his pocket. "I'm calling my lawyers. It's your choice as to whether I instruct them to start proceedings for a custody suit or to draw up a prenup and fax it through to the jet before we land in Vegas."

Gillian stared at him. He held her gaze, unflinching, unbending. Finally, she spoke. "You know my choice."

Max smiled. Perfect white teeth, cold blue eyes. "Pack your bags while I make the call. We're leaving in ten minutes and won't be back till tomorrow."

"No. We're not."

"Changed your mind already?" His thumb hovered over a button on his phone.

"No. I'm providing you with a demonstration of why you didn't, don't, want children. Ten minutes isn't enough. It's not a case of throwing a few things into a bag anymore. I'll need food for Ethan, his music, his favorite books, clothes and his blanket. I haven't showered yet myself. I'll need an hour. At least."

"I'll give you half an hour. We can buy whatever we need."

"We can't buy his favorite blanket."

"That's why I'm giving you half an hour, not ten minutes." He pressed a button on his phone, lifted it to his ear. "Tristan." He smiled at something the other man said then glanced at Gillian. "Yeah. It's important."

Dimly, she heard him talking while she made her way upstairs. This couldn't be happening. Numbly, she showered and changed and then packed.

Max said nothing when she reappeared forty-five minutes later. She stood at the doorway to the family room, two cases behind her, surveying Ethan and Max as they played trains on a completely redesigned track that now appeared to be under attack by rampaging dinosaurs.

Max scanned her from head to toe. He didn't look at his watch and he didn't say anything. She had no idea whether his lack of comment on her timekeeping was due to forbearance because of Ethan's presence, or because he'd lost track of time.

"Daddy," Ethan said, "look."

Max's eyes widened and he looked sharply back at Ethan.

She'd seen his shock. Felt it herself. "Daddy." Her son had called him "Daddy." As though for him it was the most natural thing in the world. But she knew that single word had rocked both Max's and her world to the core.

He'd never wanted children. At all, he'd said. And now a little boy was calling him "Daddy." Already making demands on him. It wasn't too late for Max to back out. Gillian held her breath.

Far from backing out, Max reached across and ruffled Ethan's curls. "Come on, tiger." Ethan seemed to swell with pride at the power of the nickname. "Mommy's waiting." He watched Gillian for her reaction. She was too numb to show any.

Out on the driveway he looked from his two-door Maserati coupe to her hatchback.

"There's not a lot of room in the back of yours for Ethan." She stated the obvious. "And his car seat and CDs are already in my car. And wipes for sticky hands." She wasn't going to feel sorry for him. This situation was of his own making. The sacrifice of driving to the airport in L.A. in her car was nothing compared to what he was asking her to do.

He shook his head. Resignation? She wasn't sure.

Lulled by the noise and the motion, Ethan was sleeping by the time the jet landed in Las Vegas. As it taxied to a halt, Max and Gillian both stood looking at him. His face and the cream leather armchair his car seat was strapped into were smudged with peanut butter, his head was tipped to one side, long lashes curling on his cheeks. Max reached for the buckles. "You take the bags," she said. "I'll take Ethan. If he wakes in someone else's arms he might get upset." Max shrugged, acquiescent now that he'd gotten his way where it counted. Or wary of getting covered in peanut butter?

Gillian crouched in front of the armchair, gently releasing the buckles. Ethan slowly opened his eyes. He smiled when he saw her and her heart swelled as it always did. "Where's Daddy?"

Gillian closed her eyes at the stab of hurt. "He's right here, sweetheart." She moved so that Ethan could see Max. She looked up at him expecting to see gloating, but what she saw was worse, and she looked away from the pity in his gaze.

In the chapel's waiting room, thoughtfully equipped with a toy box, Ethan played. Max, now wearing the dark suit he'd changed into on the jet, relaxed in one of the armchairs calmly sending emails and making and taking calls on his phone while Gillian paced the red carpet.

The door to the waiting room opened and the celebrant's assistant beckoned them. Gillian and Ethan packed up the toys. She kept hold of a book for Ethan to look at during the service, and walked to the door. She held her son's hand, hoping that he didn't sense she was, for the first time in their almost three years together, the one needing reassurance from the contact.

The assistant smiled at Gillian and patted her shoulder as she stopped in front of her. "Don't worry. Most brides are a little nervous." Gillian wasn't nervous so much as in shock. Just this morning she'd been deciding between cleaning the fridge and finishing her book. The fridge had been looking like the loser. Now the loser was her—marrying a man because of an ultimatum.

She squared her shoulders. She just needed to get through this. Max would have what he wanted—his name on a marriage certificate beside hers—and they could go home and get on with their lives.

"And you do look beautiful," said the assistant.

She glanced down at the dress that at the last minute she'd decided to bring. A silver shift dress she'd bought a couple of months ago to attend a work cocktail party with her friend Maggie. If she was going to get married, then she was going to look at least halfway decent doing it. If nothing else came of this, Ethan would have a picture of his parents marrying. She wanted to create the most realistic illusion she could. Max came to stand beside her.

"Doesn't she, sir?" The assistant looked to Max for his agreement.

"She's always *looked* lovely," he said, as though the fact bothered him.

"The two of you make a very handsome couple," the assistant continued, oblivious to the tension between them. The other woman had to be delusional if she thought they made a good couple, but maybe it helped her get pleasure from her job.

The three of them, Max, Gillian and Ethan, walked into the chapel itself. Music, a tune she didn't recognize, wafted from unseen speakers. Her heels tapped out her reluctant progress on the pale terra-cotta tiles as they made their way up the aisle between rows of white wrought-iron chairs.

"Mommy, you're holding too tight."

She eased her hold on her son's hand. "Sorry, sweetie," she whispered. If she had a bouquet she could squeeze the flowers instead. Max reached for her free hand, held it firmly. She flicked a glance in his direction, saw his frown, saw a muscle working in his jaw. But oddly, there was a strange comfort in his clasp.

She'd never been the sort to dream about her perfect wedding, but if she had, this certainly wouldn't have been it.

The marriage celebrant, a dark-haired woman in her mid-twenties, stood at the front of the room between wisteria-twined columns. "At least she's not an Elvis impersonator," Gillian murmured. The corner of Max's lips lifted.

At the front of the chapel she sat Ethan on one of the chairs, crouched in front of him and whispered for him to be good and very quiet for just a few minutes. "Why?" he asked loudly.

"I'll explain soon, okay?" She patted his knee and straightened. Her heart thudding, she walked back to Max, standing facing him. At a signal from the celebrant, the music quieted. And into the silence a little voice piped up. "Mommy, I'm hungwy."

Gillian looked at Max. The glacial blue gaze thawed to reveal suppressed amusement. "We'll get you something to eat real soon, tiger," he said. And that was enough. If it had been Gillian, the assurance would have been questioned. *What? When? But I'm hungry now.* Ethan's attention shifted to the small board book in his lap.

"We are gathered here today…" As the celebrant began to speak, Gillian tuned out the words. They meant nothing to her. She trained her gaze on the column beyond Max's shoulder.

"…on her left hand and repeat after me." Those words cut through snapping her attention back to Max.

He reached for her hand and slipped a wedding band on to her finger. He'd had the ring sent out to the jet. Born to privilege, he was the sort of man who made things happen the way he wanted.

For example, her presence here.

He passed another ring, similar but larger, to her. This ring was one of her few victories today. If she could call it that. When Max had paused during a phone call that she'd been paying no attention to, to ask her if she had any preferences in rings, she'd insisted that if she was going to wear a ring then he ought to, too. With a nod, he'd ordered two rings. A small concession on his part, but a concession nonetheless.

She repeated the words the celebrant spoke and slid the ring in question onto his finger. A part of her recognized her relief at the fact that he would be wearing a ring, too. He'd be marked as married. To her. It wasn't all one-sided.

"I now pronounce you husband and wife."

For the first time since he'd realized Ethan was his, the hard edge of tension that had seemed to grip him softened.

"You may kiss your bride."

Max's gaze met hers. Met and held. Her husband. The thought threatened to overwhelm her.

"Thank you," he said softly. Holding her hands, he leaned forward.

Too numb to do anything else, she accepted the gentle brush of his lips across hers. The memory of his capacity for tenderness surfaced.

And for just a second she closed her eyes and her own tension eased.

It was done.

His wife and son.

Max walked with Gillian and Ethan from the chapel and out into the Las Vegas sunshine.

A wife he'd married only to give their son a lawful family and to guarantee an instant part in their life.

A wife he'd expected to feel nothing for. A wife whom he'd had to restrain himself from taking in his arms and holding, because Gillian—always confident, always certain—had looked so…lost.

They crossed the cobblestone courtyard to the limousine. She held the pictures taken by the chapel's bored photographer loosely in one hand. Neither of them had looked at the photos.

He prided himself on his efficiency, on how much he managed to achieve in any given day. But finishing the day with a family, when he'd started it as a footloose, career-focused bachelor, was a major accomplishment even for him. And one he wouldn't have seen coming in a million years. He'd never intended to have a family of his own. He'd wanted to avoid the commitments and bonds that came with family. But just because it wasn't what he wanted for himself didn't mean he didn't absolutely believe in its importance.

And Ethan—his son—would have it.

He looked at the boy trotting at his side.

Without a long drawn-out battle, he'd secured a permanent and legal place in his son's life. And he'd served notice to Gillian that he wasn't going to let her shut him out.

A driver stood at the waiting vehicle and handed Gillian and a chattering Ethan into the back. Max followed. She eased herself over to the far side of the wide leather seat. The bulky car seat between them provided a physical barrier, Ethan's presence a barrier of another kind. It was probably for the best.

He was still in no mood to make nice to the woman who had deceived him, but he was getting there. There were moments, even aside from the kiss, when he forgot what lay between them and remembered the connection they'd shared, saw a glimmer of possibility for something new.

They were in this together now, and he was going to make it work.

On his terms.

She pulled a small box of raisins from her handbag and passed it to Ethan along with a slice of cheese. She looked up and caught him watching her. "You want some? I have more in my bag." She almost smiled.

Worse, he almost smiled back.

They'd had good times once. "Do we need to stop somewhere for food, or can Ethan wait till we're on the jet? There's a fully stocked galley on board."

"This will tide him over. And, Max." The way she spoke his name brought back memories. "Thanks for asking."

Max lifted a shoulder, feigning indifference. "I've only had close-up experience of one child's meltdown due to hunger and tiredness. But it was more than enough. Trust me, it's not something I'm in a hurry to repeat." For the time being he would have to take her lead on all things relating to parenting.

He adapted quickly to most any situation, but this one was so far out of left field that it was going to take some time.

Max pulled his phone from his pocket. He'd taken the first step to ensure he'd be a part of their lives. And now he had to integrate them into his.

There was one call he had to make.

He pressed speed dial. "Hi, Mom. Are you home this evening?" She started to tell him about her day. But there'd be time enough for that tonight. "If you don't have plans I thought I'd stop by for dinner." She always said he didn't come by enough, especially that he now lived back on the west coast after a stint in New York. They claimed they still barely saw him. An exaggeration. They also claimed that they didn't know what was going on in his life. Maybe not such an exaggeration.

He glanced at the seat beside him. "Oh, and I'll have a couple of people with me I want you to meet." While his mother gushed at the prospect of him bringing guests and mused over possible menus, he watched the boy studiously picking raisins from the box and chewing them one at a time. Surely it would take hours to eat that way. His gaze found Gillian, watching him, her eyebrows raised. "Don't do anything too fancy, Mom. At least one of them likes his food fairly plain." Gillian did smile then, albeit briefly. "Oh, yeah, and the other one's a woman. And yes we'll be staying the night." He finished the call.

"Staying the night? With your parents? That's not a good idea, Max." In fact, she looked like the prospect terrified her.

"We're going to be in L.A. anyway. May as well stop in and meet them. And let them meet their grandson. They're set up to have kids from all the times my sister brings her two over. And it saves Ethan an hour and a half more in the car today getting back to Vista del Mar."

She opened her mouth then closed it again. Whatever she'd been about to say, whatever excuse she'd been about to come up with, she'd realized it wasn't going to cut it. That any grounds she thought she had for protest were shaky. Instead, a few seconds later she said, "You didn't warn her. Tell her who, or what…" she lifted a shoulder in a shrug "…you were bringing."

Ethan held a raisin, which looked suspiciously like it had already been chewed, toward Max. Possibly in child etiquette, if someone offered you some of their food the correct thing to do would be to accept it. Max wasn't going there. Instead he smiled at his son. "You have it. I'm not hungry." At which, Ethan offered it to his mother and when she shook her head, popped the mangled raisin back into his mouth.

Max returned his attention to his wife. The one he was going to have to introduce to his family in almost no time at all. "It was enough that I said I was bringing a woman. She'll already be on the phone to my brothers, ordering their presence tonight. I thought the 'wife' news might be best done in person. Besides, if I wait till tonight when Dad and my brothers are there, I'll only have to explain it once."

"And how will you explain it?" She looked pale and tense. But he was not going to let himself care.

"Ethan's not going to need a whole lot of explaining. They'll know as soon as they see him that he's my son. There's a picture of me and my brother at about the same age hanging in the hallway. He's the spitting image. The hair, the eyes. Although I'm fairly sure I never offered people my half-eaten raisins. And as for you, I'll think of something."

She twisted the gold band on her left hand. "I never met your family when we were dating. You scarcely even talked about them."

"I know." The omission had been deliberate. He liked to keep the different areas of his life separate. Introducing a woman to his parents could lead to her getting the wrong impression. And vice versa. He'd never brought any of the women he'd dated home to meet his family.

His parents had a good marriage and were keen for their children, and particularly Max, to have that same emotional closeness with someone else. So keen that Max had learned at an early age not to even let on when he was dating someone. Particularly when he'd never had any intention of making it serious. Because as fervently as they wished he'd find that bond, he avoided it. They wouldn't like the fact that he'd just married a woman that not only had they never met, but who he didn't love. It would only upset them. "They're not to know why we've married."

"You mean your ultimatum?"

"Or your willful deception." That took the wind out of her sails. She looked out the window, seemingly intrigued by their approach to the Las Vegas airport. "I want them to think ours is a real marriage." He watched the back of her head. He'd always liked her hair, liked running his fingers through it. "A marriage based on love." Her spine stiffened.

She turned back to him. "And what you want, you get?"

She'd always challenged him. Apparently, unwillingly, he still admired that about her.

"Mommy?" Ethan's voice was plaintive.

"It's all right, honey." She stroked their son's curls back from his forehead. "Don't worry, Max," she said quietly. "You'll get no argument from me. At least not in public. But just so you know, I'll be doing it for Ethan's sake, not yours."

"I expected nothing more. You've made it clear that my feelings aren't something you take into consideration."

She drew in a sharp breath. "Max, I…"

He waited, curious to see whether she'd go on the offense or defense. He was ready for either.

She took the cheese wrapper Ethan held out for her, took her time folding it up and tucking it into a small plastic bag from within her handbag. She looked back at him, her composure regained. "If your parents are going to think we're happily married then I need to know something about them. Like, for starters, their names." She opened the shoulder bag that he was beginning to view as something akin to a magician's hat. "Because if our marriage is based on love then we'll have talked about our families." As she rummaged in its depths, her hair swung forward, glossy and inviting, curtaining her face, hiding the lips he'd so recently kissed. He wanted to brush it back.

Ethan, his thoughts in sync with Max's, reached for her hair. Ethan's execution, though, was somewhat different to what Max had been thinking. His little fist closed around a handful of hair and he pulled as he giggled.

"Ethan, no." Gillian tried to turn her head but Ethan held firm and giggled louder. "Ethan. Let go of my hair." He giggled some more, his fingers now well and truly tangled.

Max reached over and held his laughing son's wrist steady while he unwound Gillian's hair from around his fingers.

"He's not usually a hair puller," she said when she was able to straighten. "Thank you."

"A pleasure." And it had been, touching her hair again, every bit as soft and silky as he remembered. "Except for the raisiny bits."

She smiled as she ran her fingers through the recently pulled hair, smoothing it back into place, and something tenuous and beguiling shimmered between them as she held his gaze. He remembered so much more about her than just her hair.

Returning her attention to her bag, she produced a small plastic car for Ethan and then a notebook and pen. She held her pen, poised above the paper. "Your parents' names?"

"Stephen and Laura. My sister's Kristan, and my brothers are Daniel, Jake and Carter."

She looked up, her face paler than it had been seconds ago. "Are they all going to be there?"

Was that apprehension in those earnest green eyes? "Surely the formidable Gillian Mitchell isn't worried about meeting a few people?"

"Of course not." She lifted her chin. "It was a simple question. Are they all going to be there? It impacts how much I need to know now."

"All except Kristan and her family, and Daniel."

"And your other brothers, are they all like you?"

"In what way?"

"Career-focused, forthright, suspicious, emotionally shut down?"

"You could be describing yourself."

She frowned and then the creases vanished. "Maybe that's how I used to be. But I've changed, Max. I had to."

He wasn't going to ask if the intervening years had been hard for her. Not when she'd denied him the opportunity of helping, of even being there. But he'd noticed some of the changes in her. There was a softer edge to her, a nurturing side he'd been unaware of. Even physically she looked softer, curvier. And he would not think about exploring those changes. Just this morning he'd told her she'd killed any attraction he could have ever felt for her. And he needed that to be true.

He'd married her because he was determined to be a part of his son's life and that his son would grow up with a father who was married to his mother. And despite his threat to win custody of Ethan, he wouldn't have been able to do that to the boy. Or even to Gillian.

She shifted in her seat, crossed one leg over the other then tugged the silver skirt of her dress down from where it had ridden up her thighs.

But it was turning out that the attraction he'd once felt was far from dead. Contrary to his efforts and intentions, a heartbeat, faint but steady and insistent, was registering.

Four

Back in L.A. after the flight, Max negotiated the imposing, palm-lined Beverly Hills streets, and Gillian scanned her notes, doing her best to tune out her awareness of Max's proximity.

All the while also trying to tune out the memory of the touch of his lips to hers. A touch that had brought back a flood of sensual recollections, a touch that had tapped into some kind of primal programming to this man and what her body knew of him. She reread her notes. There would be time to analyze that ill-advised kiss later, to try to somehow reprogram her responses.

Confident that she'd learned the details, she flipped her notebook closed and put her memory to the test. She held up her thumb. "Carter's the oldest. Serious, shorter than you but same color hair and eyes, runs a software company, recently separated from his fiancée. Like most of your family, supports the Dodgers." She looked to Max for confirmation—avoiding his lips. He nodded for her to continue.

She tore her gaze from his face and held up her first finger. She had forgotten the sheer magnetism of him. "Daniel's next but won't be here. Neither will Kristan." Thankfully. She figured there would be enough of his siblings to cope with as it was.

She lifted her second finger. "Jake, younger than you, same height, green eyes, rebel of the family, tried modeling and then acting, successful at both and has since surprised everyone by swapping sides of the camera to become even more successful as a film director. Supports the Angels, leading to much good-natured, though I'm guessing heated, rivalry and dinner table discussions."

"You always were good with details."

"Thank you." Although she didn't think he'd meant it as a compliment, more a statement of fact. And she so wasn't looking forward to fronting up to two more versions of Max.

"Mom and Dad?"

"Laura loves gardening and her charity work. She's cultured and reserved and can come across as a little aloof, but there's a chance she'll warm to me. And Stephen made his money in property development, plays golf and enjoys single-malt whiskey and, surprise, surprise, watching baseball."

"You'll pass." Max turned into the drive, pressed a code into a keypad and as the gates swung slowly open, eased through them.

They swept past stately oaks to a wide circular driveway and stopped in front of an imposing two-story home. Gillian clasped her hands together and took a deep breath. "It's easy enough to do sitting here in the car, but—"

"You'll be fine."

He could have dismissed or ignored her concern but there

was reassurance in his tone, and in his brief glance. They got out of the car and flicked their seat backs forward for access to the rear. Gillian looked from the previously pristine backseat of Max's Maserati to his face. In the space of the thirty-minute drive from the airport Ethan had managed to strew quite some mess. "I did suggest my car," she said. "Just imagine what he can do on a long trip."

"I dread to think."

By the time she straightened with Ethan in her arms, the front door of the house had opened to reveal a slim woman, wearing tailored pants and a lilac cardigan—Gillian guessed cashmere. Her silver-blond hair curved precisely below her chin. Max came round to Gillian's side. "Your mother?" she asked.

"Yes. Let me take your bag. I'm starting to realize it must weigh a ton."

She dropped her shoulder to let him ease it from her. He tested its weight experimentally, then, holding it in one hand, put his free arm about her shoulders, his warmth surrounding and supporting. "Let's do this." For the first time it felt not as though she was alone against Max but as though he was on her side and they were facing something together.

They walked toward the front door. His mother's gaze was firmly fixed on Gillian and Ethan. She was smiling, but the effect was diminished by a puzzled frown pleating her brow. By the time they stood under the portico, Laura had given up any pretense of smiling and was staring openly at Ethan.

"Hi, Mom." Max released Gillian's shoulder long enough to kiss his mother's cheek. "You're looking terrific."

"Max?" The word sounded strangled and Gillian felt for the other woman.

Max stood back beside Gillian and slid his arm around her waist and she was grateful for that show of support, not only because she desperately needed the assurance it offered, but because he could have made this difficult for her. More difficult, she mentally corrected. There was no way this was going to be easy. "I want you to meet Gillian and Ethan. Gillian, this is my mother, Laura."

Laura dragged her gaze from Ethan to smile at Gillian, but the smile faltered and she looked back at Ethan. "Max?"

"I've got some news for you, Mom. Let's go inside."

Laura recalled herself and stepped back. "Of course, come in. You've just driven up from Vista del Mar?"

"Actually, no. We've just flown in from Las Vegas."

Laura's eyes widened and her gaze darted to Gillian's left hand where it was tucked around Ethan, supporting his weight, and then to Max's hand. His wedding ring glinted. "Stephen," she called, a faint plea for help registering in the word. Though she'd spoken so quietly that Stephen, wherever he was, couldn't possibly have heard.

"Why don't we go sit down," Max prompted gently. With a glance back at Gillian and Ethan, Laura led the way through the house to a spacious, high-ceilinged living room.

Three men, all of them big, were sprawled on low, wheat-colored couches, their attention riveted on an enormous flat-screen television. It was easy enough to pick out Stephen, their father, and Max had given her good enough descriptions that Gillian was fairly certain she knew which brother was which.

Laura cleared her throat. "Max and his…friends are here."

Only one of the men, Jake, Gillian guessed, glanced their way before the play was up. His observant gaze lit on Gillian and Ethan and froze there.

"Stephen. Turn the TV off." Laura instructed quietly.

"This better be good, Max," the man next to Stephen—had to be Carter, Gillian figured—muttered as their father pressed mute on a remote.

"It's good all right," Jake said, a broad smile spreading across his face as he levered himself off the couch. "Real good."

The two others stood and all three men crossed toward Gillian and Max, like an approaching forest of oaks.

"Dad, guys," Max said as his father got to them first, "this is Gillian and Ethan." Gillian readjusted Ethan on her hip and reached to shake the hand Stephen held out to her. "Do you want me to take Ethan?" Max asked her quietly.

Ethan heard the offer, smiled and reached for Max. "Daddy." The word rang clear and loud in the quiet living room. The silence stretched till it was broken by Jake's roar of laughter. Ethan, still leaning toward Max and delighted to have caused such merriment, repeated his trick. "Daddy, Daddy, Daddy." Soon the boom of the two brothers' laughter filled the room. Their parents didn't share their amusement.

Gillian met Max's gaze over Ethan's head. A trace of wry amusement sparkled in his blue eyes. "I guess that's one explanation taken off my hands," he said. He reached for Ethan but the noise had gotten to her son, who changed his mind and clung like a limpet to Gillian instead, burying his face in her shoulder.

"And before Ethan beats me to my second announcement, you ought to know that Gillian is your sister-in-law, and daughter-in-law," he added with a nod in his parents' direction.

Did that mean he didn't want to call her his wife? She didn't blame him.

"You always were the secretive one. How long have you been married?" Jake asked, having gotten his amusement under control.

Max glanced at his watch. "In minutes as well as hours?"

Jake filled the silence that yawned after that pronouncement. "We didn't get an invite?"

"It wasn't that sort of wedding."

That simple statement quelled any lingering amusement. Laura stepped into the breach. "Welcome to the family, Gillian." She kissed Gillian's cheek. "And welcome to you, too, Ethan." She planted a quick kiss on Ethan's curls. "Why don't we all sit down and get to know one another. We have half an hour before dinner's ready."

Half an hour of interrogation, Gillian suspected from the questioning looks on everyone's faces. Oh, goody. The only saving grace was that many of the questions would undoubtedly be directed at Max. And the fact that Ethan was here would surely be a kind of buffer and icebreaker as well.

"Hey, buddy," Jake said to Ethan. "Want to come with your uncle Jake to choose a toy to play with? My nieces have a whole room full of them here."

"I don't think so," Gillian said. "He's quite shy around strangers."

"Yes, please." Ethan immediately made a liar of her and wriggled out of her hold and down her body. "Have they got a twain?"

He trotted off with Jake, who tossed a wink back over his shoulder at her. "We'll be back in a minute."

Laura watched them go. "How old is he?"

"Nearly three," Gillian said.

"His birthday's the same as mine," Max said quietly.

Laura swung sharply back to look at Max, an expression on her face Gillian couldn't interpret. Shock? Pain? It was so quickly replaced by neutrality that Gillian almost thought she'd imagined it. Laura gestured to the closest couch. "Sit down. Tell us a little about yourself."

"Mom." Max's voice held a note of warning.

"I just want to talk to my new daughter-in-law," Laura said innocently. "Stephen, I think you should turn that off."

Stephen's glance had strayed to the muted TV. "I was just thinking the same thing myself." With a last lingering glance at the screen he pressed a button on the remote and the screen went blank.

Gillian lowered herself to the couch, grateful when Max sat next to her, and even more grateful when he took her hand in his. She tightened her grip around his.

"What is it you do, Gillian?" She knew there were plenty more questions that Laura would undoubtedly want answers to, like why was she only now meeting her almost three-year-old grandson, so Gillian was thankful for the casually polite question.

"I'm a journalist with a paper in Vista del Mar."

"The *Seaside Gazette*," Max added.

"Isn't that the paper that's been—" Carter cut himself short.

"The paper that's been the thorn in my side?" Max asked. "Yes."

Gillian could just imagine how Max might have complained about the *Gazette* to his family.

"But Gillian and I have always kept our personal and professional relationships separate."

Just like in L.A. Though they'd met because of the intersections between their careers, they'd strenuously kept their work out of their relationship. In fact, they'd kept almost everything out of their relationship except the physical passion that had flamed between them. She'd been new to L.A. at the time and had thought she had to be sophisticated and unemotional. She'd thought she could play it that way. So they'd had good times, but neither of them had made an effort to truly know the other. They thought they'd had the relationship the way they wanted it, the way it ought to be. Superficial and fun. When Gillian made the shocking discovery that she was pregnant and realized she wanted more and hinted as much to Max, he'd ended it. She couldn't blame him.

"But I have the highest respect for her integrity, even if I occasionally think it's misguided."

Gillian hadn't expected the compliment, but she knew that at least at one time it had been true. Before they'd ended up on opposite sides of the fence regarding Cameron Enterprises' takeover of Worth Industries.

"And what is it your folks do?"

"My mom owns a store up near Fort Bragg, and I never really knew my father. I have no idea what he does."

Laura opened her mouth but it was a second or two before any words came out. "What sort of store?"

"A kind of art gallery."

Laura brightened. "Perhaps we know it."

Gillian looked at the sculptures and oil paintings in the living room and tried to imagine some of the things her mother sold—paintings of other dimensions, of spirit guides and angels hanging here. "Probably not," she said. "It's a small shop, very new age."

"Oh."

Gillian racked her brain for something else to say. Usually she could talk easily to anyone. But there were too many conversational minefields here for her to know which direction to go in. Fortunately, at that moment Ethan came trotting back, clutching a small stack of books, Jake following. "No *twain,*" Jake said. "Only dolls and books. Books won. But I've promised him a train before his next visit."

"Uncle Jake's never forgiven Mom for passing his train set on to the neighbor's kid," Carter said. "When he was twenty. He's been looking for an excuse to get another one ever since." The brothers laughed, the sound warm and inclusive.

Ethan had grown up without extended family. Now he had a father, grandparents, an aunt and a swag of uncles and cousins.

Gillian was torn between guilt that she'd denied her son this and terror that he'd grow to like it only to have it taken away when Max realized that he'd been right when he'd insisted that marriage and children weren't things he wanted or needed.

Jake resumed his seat on the couch. Ethan climbed up beside him and passed him a book about a little yellow digger.

All Gillian had ever wanted was to do the very best she could for her son.

And she still didn't know what that was.

She looked at Max. In a room practically brimming with charismatic men, Max was still the one who riveted her attention, who made her pulse pick up. It was his eyes that caught and held her gaze, the hint of pain walled off, the unfathomable depths in them, the intelligence and decency they hinted at.

And passion. The one area he'd never held back from her.

His hand tightened around hers and the remembrance of that passion flickered.

Gillian felt it in the pit of her stomach, felt it bring color to her cheeks. Her physical response was as unexpected as it was unwanted. She didn't, couldn't, wouldn't still feel anything for Max. It was the only way she'd be able to survive this marriage.

"How long have you been in Vista del Mar?" Laura asked.

Max, still looking at her, lifted an eyebrow, sharing the fact that he, too, didn't know the answer.

"Six months," she said to him, then turned to Laura. "I love it there. It's a wonderful place to raise a child."

"More importantly, Dodgers or Angels?" Jake interrupted his storytelling to ask.

Gillian shook her head. "I've heard about the divided

loyalties in this family and there's no way I'm getting drawn into it."

"She's Angels," Max announced on her behalf.

"I knew I liked you," Jake said with a smile and a glance of triumph sent Carter's way, before turning back to the book he was reading to Ethan.

Conversation limped along for ten more minutes till Laura excused herself to check on dinner, suggesting as she left that Max show Gillian their and Ethan's rooms.

Leaving Ethan engrossed in the next story Jake was reading, Gillian headed up the stairs behind Max. They didn't speak as he led her along the hallway, finally stopping at an open door. "This will be Ethan's room. It's a bit girly because it's been set up for my nieces. We'll get some stuff in here for Ethan."

"I don't think I should be away from him tonight. It's his first night here." There were twin beds, she'd happily sleep in one of them.

Max crossed the room and opened another door to reveal an adjoining room dominated by a king-size bed. He stepped back so Gillian could enter. "This is our bedroom. We can leave the door between the two open."

"Our?"

Five

Gillian's throat ran dry as she stared at the lushly draped king-size bed and the implications rained down on her.

She hadn't thought it possible for things to get any worse. She'd been wrong. The trouble was she'd had all she could do to keep up with the present moment as the day lurched and leaped from crisis to calamity. She hadn't thought ahead.

"Yes, our, but don't worry, I won't touch you." His voice was cool, any hint of the remembered heat she thought she'd seen earlier had gone. "The bed's big enough. We have to share because my parents will already have enough doubts about our sudden marriage. I'm not giving them any further cause for concern. We'll be doing things together like a normal couple, like a normal family."

Too much, too fast.

How could she be expected to share a bed with him, a man she'd once had such a passionate relationship with, a man she'd once hoped could love her? How did they pretend to be normal parents, with a normal relationship in public, while in private he could look so coldly at her?

He demonstrated how after dinner.

The meal had been pleasant, if she ignored the underlying strain of tension and the occasional looks she caught among Max's family, but they made an effort to welcome her. And Max had been warm and affectionate. She could almost believe he meant it. Within his family he was different, though even from them he seemed to hold something of himself back.

His parents and brothers were nice people. People who in other circumstances she would have been completely relaxed around.

As it was, she was glad of the excuse of needing to bathe Ethan when she stood from the table. She hid her surprise when Max stood, too.

Together they knelt at the side of the bath while Ethan splashed and played with the bath toys, keeping up a stream of chatter. But the silence between them, as they shared this simple parenting task, was almost companionable.

Ethan dive-bombed a little red tugboat into the bath, sending up a fountain of water that splashed both Max and her, soaking their fronts. Before she'd realized it they were laughing together.

"Not your usual Saturday night?" Gillian asked as their laughter quieted and she eyed the shirt plastered to the contours of his chest.

Max's gaze softened on her. "No. This is a first for me. And to be honest, if anyone had asked, I would have said I couldn't think of anything I'd less like to do, but right now there isn't anywhere in the world I'd rather be."

Gillian looked away and studied her hands dangling over the rim of the bubble-filled bath. "I'm sorry for not telling you."

Ethan made motor noises as he pushed the tugboat around,

driving it into a duck and then a dragon. Finally, thinking he wasn't going to answer, she glanced at Max. His blue eyes were so serious. "I don't know if I can forgive you for it but…I can understand why you did it. After what I'd said. What I believed at the time. And knowing how I would have reacted."

She shrugged. His concession was more than she'd expected.

And maybe it was a place they could move forward from.

At Gillian's prompting, Ethan stood and she reached for a towel, wrapping him in it.

"I'll lift him out if you like," Max offered. "You'll get wet. Wetter."

"So will you."

"I don't mind if my brothers can see through *my* shirt. You on the other hand…"

She looked down at the green blouse she'd changed into earlier. She'd been so distracted by the contours of Max's chest that she'd forgotten to consider her own *contours,* and the way the pale cotton would cling.

"Oh." The heat of a blush crept up her face. Ridiculous since Max had seen way more of her than the outline of her breasts. But that was then and that was different. "Thanks."

He lifted Ethan from the water. Together they readied him for bed, dressing him in his pajamas, then Max carried him to his bedroom. They tucked him in and sat on the side of Ethan's bed for a few minutes before Max, realizing Gillian's desire to be alone for a while, kissed his son good-night and left. In the doorway he turned back, his gaze soft on them before walking down the hallway.

With just a night-light for illumination, Gillian looked at her little boy as his eyelids drifted closed. He was so like his father. She shook her head. For a few minutes this morning she'd thought today was going to be an ordinary Saturday.

And now her whole world had been turned upside down.

She was married to Max, a man who didn't love her, but who she could only hope would grow to love Ethan and be there for him for the long haul. If being married to him helped ensure that, she had to at least try to be glad of it.

Not frightened.

She wasn't even sure what the fear was about. She trusted Max. He had a deep integrity. He'd said going into their original relationship what he did and didn't want. So if he said he wouldn't touch her, he wouldn't.

The fear came from watching his tenderness with Ethan, and wanting some of it for herself. She'd cared for Max once, more than she'd let on because she'd known he didn't want that from her. She had to be stronger than to care for him again.

She'd learned to live with loneliness, without his presence or warmth. She could go on without it now.

With Ethan asleep she had no excuse to linger up here so she made her way downstairs, pausing near the bottom when she heard her name. The sound came from the home office she'd noticed off the entry.

"I'm not the only one of us with a hell of a lot of questions." Carter's low voice carried to her.

Her hand tightened on the banister.

"Keep them to yourself because if they're about Gillian and me they're none of your damn business." Max's tone was mild but unbending.

"If she's after the Preston wealth then they are my business."

She should keep moving or make some kind of sound so that they knew she was nearby.

"She's not." Max's words were clipped.

"Just tell me she signed a prenup?"

Max paused. "Yes."

"I hope it's iron-clad. You're worth a fortune. It's pretty tempting."

"Don't worry about it, Carter. She's not like that." Max defended her. Now there was a surprise. "I can guarantee she didn't marry me for my money." Gillian almost smiled. That much was definitely true. Max had mentioned that Carter's engagement had ended when he'd discovered his fiancée was more interested in his wealth than him. So his cynicism was understandable.

"She's pretty and everything. I'll give you that. And she seems nice," Carter said, still not sounding convinced.

"She is nice." There was a warning edge to Max's voice. "And yes, she's pretty, but she's also honest and kind and has the courage of her convictions. She always stands up for the underdog. That spirit was the thing that first drew me to her."

Carter laughed.

"Okay." Max's voice softened and Gillian thought she heard a hint of amusement. "Maybe it was the second thing. But trust me on this, Carter, I know what I'm doing."

"You usually do, but this seems to have come out of nowhere."

Gillian held her breath. What would Max say to that? Because for him it really had come out of nowhere, approximately twelve hours ago. How much would he tell his brother?

"If Ethan didn't look so much like you and Dylan at the same age…" Carter said.

Dylan? Gillian frowned. She mentally reviewed the names of the siblings Max had given her. There'd been no mention of a Dylan in the family. Perhaps a cousin?

"But he does look like me, exactly like me, so let's drop

this." His tone had changed again, the warning edge back and sharper than before.

She didn't want to be the cause of disharmony between the brothers. Gillian backed up a step or two and let her heels click on the stairs as she walked down and past the office door on her way to the living room. Max and Carter entered a few seconds after her.

Stephen offered her a drink but Gillian declined. "I know it's early but it's been a long day. I think I'll go to bed, too." She'd go to bed and hopefully be sound asleep before Max came up.

"Of course," said Jake, smiling, who then looked at Max. "It's your wedding night. I guess you'll both be wanting an early night."

Max rested his hand on Gillian's shoulder and she almost jumped at the touch. Her nerves were strung so tight she'd be lucky if she slept at all tonight. His hand firmed, his thumb rubbed at the tense muscle beneath it and a knowing gleam lit his eyes as he looked at her. "Yeah. We'll both say goodnight." If she didn't know better she could almost believe... She mentally shook her head. She did know better.

They left the room together. Walked up the stairs side by side. Without the distraction of Ethan's presence to divert attention from where they were going, or disguise the tension between them, the silence felt fraught. They entered the room they were to spend the night in.

Alone together.

In bed.

Gillian racked her brain for something to say. Something to break that silence. Could she ask about Dylan? It would be a distraction but not, she guessed, a welcome one. Plus it would reveal that she had overheard his conversation with his brother. And she didn't want him thinking she'd been eavesdropping. Even though, she admitted, she had been.

"You take the first shower," Max said. "I've got some things I need to do." Okay, she didn't need to worry about providing a distraction. He crossed to the bag he'd brought from the jet, pulled out a laptop and, dropping on to the bed, stretched out his legs, opened the computer and started tapping at keys. "We'll head back to Vista del Mar straight after breakfast tomorrow," he said without so much as looking up.

Relief that he was suddenly all business welled. Relief and a flicker of…was it disappointment?

Gillian showered and changed into her pajamas—the only proper nightwear she had—taking as much time as she could, but eventually she had no option left but to take a deep breath and walk back out into the bedroom. And see what happened next. How would he be? Remote was good, she decided. Remote was safe.

Ready to meet Max's cool gaze with distant one of her own, she stopped short when she saw him. He sat on the broad bed, propped up against the pillows, his laptop open on his lap but his head tipped back and his eyes closed. She permitted herself this unguarded moment to study him. Asleep he looked even more like Ethan, his dark lashes kissing his high cheekbones, his face softened. Asleep was even safer than remote.

Except that watching him like this made something tender within her soften in response. The unfastened top buttons of his shirt revealed a deep vee of skin.

Gillian tiptoed to the far side of the bed and lifted the covers up just enough that she could slip beneath them, pulling the crisp sheets up to her chin. She lay straight, arms by her sides, and only then chanced a glance at Max.

His eyes were only half-closed now and a small smile played about his lips. "What?" she demanded.

"Frightened of waking me?"

"No," she lied.

His smile vanished and a glimmer lit his eyes. The trouble was he knew her too well. He'd always been able to read her.

Before, that hadn't been a problem.

He closed his laptop and stood. For long seconds he considered her. And in complete contrast to his ability to read her, Gillian had no idea whatsoever what he was thinking. Finally, he crossed to the bathroom and stopped. Turning off the bedroom light, he stood silhouetted by the light from the bathroom. Broad shoulders, lean hips. "Nice pj's, by the way," he said, before pulling the door shut behind him.

Nice pj's? Way to show her maturity. Lemon-yellow with dancing bears. Ethan had helped her choose them. Still, it was surely better than the skimpy, silky nightwear Max had so enjoyed her wearing previously.

She lay in bed trying to sleep, but instead fixated on the sounds of Max, the running of the tap as he brushed his teeth, the rush of water as he showered. She remembered his routines. Tried to stop herself visualizing.

The scent of him, clean and male, as he slipped into bed beside her in the darkened room, was tantalizingly familiar and brought back memories all of its own.

He never used to wear anything to bed. *Please let that have changed. Please let him be wearing a lovely thick pair of blue striped flannel pajamas. And woolly socks.* She didn't want an accidentally outstretched hand in the night to encounter the warmth of his bare skin. She folded her arms across her chest, crossed her legs at the ankles, and held herself still, aware of every breath in the darkness.

"Good night, Gillian." His voice was low and seductive.

"Good night." Hers was little better than a squeak. It was going to be a long night.

A long night for her at least. But apparently not for him. Within minutes Max's breathing slowed and deepened. Asleep already? Was he completely unaffected by her presence,

her nearness? She should be grateful but it was almost…
insulting.

She rolled onto her side, presenting her back to him as
she readjusted her pillow. Sleep would come eventually but
it wouldn't be anytime soon. Not for her.

Somewhere in the small hours of the night, a whimpering
voice calling "Mommy" woke her. She climbed from the bed
and hurried through to Ethan's room, sitting on the side of
his bed to stroke his head and reassure him. He wasn't even
fully awake, he'd been calling out from the depths of a dream,
and her voice and touch were enough to settle him back to a
calmer sleep. If only it was that easy for her. Reluctantly, she
rose to return to the other bedroom and froze.

Max stood blocking the doorway.

Boxers.

The dim, orange illumination of Ethan's night-light was
enough to show her that. Dark boxers. And an unfortunate
expanse of contoured chest and torso. Muscle and skin.
Shadows and light.

"He's okay?" he asked.

"Fine." She walked slowly toward him, stopping in front
of him. Near enough to feel his warmth.

"Does he do that often?"

She glanced back at Ethan. "Occasionally."

Max hesitated. "Was it hard?" he asked softly. "Doing it
all on your own?" He lifted his hand and brushed a lock of
her hair back behind her ear. Fingertips skimming her jaw.
The gesture tender and almost intimate. She could want that
touch. If she let herself.

Gillian swallowed. "It wasn't easy."

"Did you ever think of calling me?" His hand came to
rest on her shoulder. As though he, too, wanted this simple
connection to last.

"Yes." Every day. Sometimes every hour. "But you didn't want this."

"No," he agreed.

"It was lonely sometimes." She'd never admitted that to anyone; she'd wanted to cope perfectly, thought that would validate her decision. But it hadn't stopped her thinking of him, missing him.

"There's been no one else?"

Did she imagine a slight tension in that hand on her shoulder? "No." There had been neither the time nor the inclination. She'd devoted all her energies to her son and her job. And after the bewilderment and pain she'd endured at the end of her relationship with Max, his unceremonious dumping of her, she'd not even had any desire to go back to the potential hurt, not to mention the complications of a relationship. The loneliness was a small price to pay to protect her son and her heart. But beneath it all she'd missed Max. Missed having him to share the moments like this with.

"You've done a good job. He's a great kid."

The compliment, the shared pride, warmed her. "Thank you, though I don't know how much credit I can take. He came out good. Settled and happy from the beginning. I was lucky."

"I'd say that part came from you." His hand shifted on her shoulder, warm and firm.

"Maybe. But his determination to do things his own way, I think that came from you."

She caught the gleam of white teeth as his lips eased into a smile. Exactly the kind of shared moment she'd never had.

"Will you get back to sleep okay? You weren't always good at that." The question was harmless but his voice low and warm wrapped itself around her in the same way his hand curved around her neck.

Too clearly, she remembered the best way Max had

discovered for helping her achieve the boneless completion that led to sleep. "I've gotten better with practice." What she clearly hadn't gotten better at was controlling her reaction to this man. Even now, when she should know better she wanted to reach out, just to touch her fingers to his chest, to see if he felt like he used to, a pleasure to her senses. Solid and warm… male.

The air seemed to shimmer and hum between them. Drawn to him, she leaned closer. She shouldn't want his touch, shouldn't want his arms around her. But he was the father of her child, and she had shared more of herself with this man than any other person.

In the dim light, his gaze dipped to her lips. She held her breath, her heartbeat heavy in her chest. Time stretched.

He took a sudden step back and turned from her.

Six

Max woke, knowing something was different. He turned his head and saw that difference sleeping beside him. Gillian.

He had a wife.

In his bed.

Breathing softly. Her lips full and rosy. Lips he'd kissed yesterday. Lips he'd kissed three years ago. Lips he'd kissed in his dreams.

During the night, she'd moved closer to the center. And so, somehow, had he. She lay on her side, facing him, within easy touching distance. Her chestnut hair spilled over her pillow, one lock sweeping across her pale cheek. A storm surge of erotic memories and unwanted desire rushed through him.

His weakness for her dismayed him. By rights he should still be furious, but he couldn't quite hold on to the anger. Maybe because he also didn't seem able to rein in his attraction for her. Worse, he knew she still felt it, too. Though she did her best to hide it. The awareness, the remembered desire, had passed between them in the quiet stillness last night.

He didn't want to want her. And he wasn't going to be the first to admit or give in to that wanting. That was why he'd turned from her last night when instinct had screamed otherwise.

But that was then. This was now. She was close and warm and soft. He curled his hands into fists before they reached to stroke that lock of hair from her cheek. "Morning." He made the word gruff. Waking her so that he wouldn't be the one lying here thinking about her touch, about the feel of her beneath him.

Slowly, her eyes opened, then widened farther as the first shock of seeing him registered. Her lush lips parted. Again, unable to stop the recollections, he remembered what those lips could do, the pleasure they could bring.

Time hung suspended.

She sucked in a breath, snapped her jaw shut and scooted to the far side of the bed, rolling on to her back and sitting up a little against the pillows. Avoiding his gaze, she looked around the room. "So what happens now?" she asked, all brisk and businesslike.

Despite his intentions the wrong answer slid into his mind. Along with the awareness that just because he wasn't going to let her anywhere near his heart didn't mean their bodies had to miss out.

Neither of them might be ready to admit or explore the possibilities between them just yet. But they were married now and would be spending a lot of time, a lot of nights, together.

Her proximity sent a renewed surge of desire sweeping through him. He wouldn't allow it. Not now. "What time does Ethan wake?"

Gillian glanced at the bedside clock. "Anytime now."

"In that case, we get up and dressed so we can get on the road back to Vista del Mar as soon as possible."

She nodded, still not looking at him. "Dibs on the bathroom?"

"It's all yours."

Eager to put distance between them, she slid from beneath the covers and stood in her dancing bear pajamas, her hair disheveled and falling softly over her shoulders. A soft tap sounded on the door. "Room service," Jake called through the door. "You two decent?"

"Give us a moment," Max called. "Get back into bed," he whispered to Gillian, who stood at the side of the bed as though frozen to the spot.

She slipped once more between the sheets, sitting back against the pillows on the very edge of the bed. Max shook his head. "Closer to me. And completely beneath the covers."

"He'll think I haven't got anything on."

"That's the general idea. Sure as heck beats him seeing the dancing bears and knowing we didn't make love on our wedding night."

She edged closer till she was almost touching him. Max closed the little remaining distance till her side pressed along his. The soft yellow fabric of her pajamas didn't provide anywhere near the barrier it ought. "It's still not right," he whispered. "You look like a nun. Undo the first couple of buttons and slip your shoulders from your top."

"But—"

"Just do it."

She bit her lip and wriggled around beneath the sheet, finally settling the covers back into place with just a glimpse of the tops of her bare, pale shoulders showing. Warmth. Heat. Desire. And it was only a glimpse of shoulder.

The part of him that was no better than a teenager governed by hormones wanted Jake in Timbuktu and that top and those bottoms off her completely.

But, he reminded himself, he wasn't a teenager. He was a

grown man, in control of his choices and his actions. Even if he wasn't totally in control of all of his body parts. Thank goodness for the thick comforter on the bed. "Come in," he called.

Jake pushed open the door and stepped in carrying a laden tray. "Not looking at anything," he said, his gaze averted. "Mom wanted me to bring this up. Don't blame me. I told her it was a bad idea but she insisted."

"Tell her thanks, but she shouldn't have," Max said with feeling. "And for goodness' sakes, look where you're going before you walk through Gillian's underwear strewn about the floor."

"It's not!"

He slipped an arm around her rigid shoulder, his hand resting half on flannel and half on bare skin. And if it hadn't been for the distraction and presence of his brother he could almost have been undone. It had been too long since he'd had a woman. Too long since he'd had *this* woman.

Jake finally glanced their way and set the tray down on the nearest bedside table. "Just acting on my orders. Your orders, on the other hand, are to enjoy your breakfast and take your time coming down. Ethan's already up and having breakfast. We'll look after him and bring him to you if he wants you."

Max wouldn't have thought it possible, but Gillian tensed even further beneath his touch. "I don't think that's such a good idea." Her son was her buffer between them, her excuse to divert her attention. If he was happily ensconced with his uncles and grandparents she had no excuses left.

"I'm only the messenger." Jake held his hands up, palms facing them. He backed from the room. "Enjoy. And, barring emergencies, I promise no more interruptions." He winked at them before pulling the door shut behind him.

Gillian wriggled her arms and shoulders fully back into

her pajama top at the same time as she scooted away from him. Any farther and she'd fall off the edge.

He wanted her back.

"So now what?" she asked.

Max glanced at the tray. "Now, coffee or OJ, and eggs benedict by the look of it."

"Really?"

"Mom asked me last night what your favorite breakfast was."

"You remembered?"

"It's not a big deal." Was it a sign of weakness that he remembered so very much more about her than her favorite breakfast? That though he told himself he'd wiped her from his life and his mind, he clearly hadn't?

"Thank you."

He poured two cups of coffee from the silver coffeepot, and once she'd levered herself to sitting, handed her one.

They ate in silence. She'd always been comfortable with his silences, not feeling the need to fill a void. She was easy to be with in that way.

From the corner of his eye he watched her cut delicate portions of her breakfast and chew slowly. A crumb from her English muffin fell down the vee of her top. She pulled the top out from her chest and fished for it. Too late, Max returned his attention to his own breakfast. He'd seen the luscious swell of breast, glimpsed a darkened peak. And his body had responded. Fiercely.

He'd dated a few women since Gillian. Had let none of the relationships become serious. Had let none of them get to the point of sharing breakfast in bed. But breakfast in bed was something of a Preston family tradition, as evidenced by this morning's room service. And he'd occasionally done the same for Gillian in their time together. Bringing her breakfast, which they'd eaten sitting in bed, occasionally reading the paper, but more often following up the meal with long lazy lovemaking.

Definitely the paper today. They had to kill at least forty minutes up here, if not longer, in order not to raise his family's suspicions. He finished his eggs, reached for the newspaper, pulled off the sports section for himself and put the remaining paper on the bed between them. True to form, she reached for the section containing the comics and puzzles. She folded it to reveal the crossword and pulled a pen from her bag on the floor.

In the old days she'd consulted him over the puzzle if she came across a difficult clue. Today she was silent, chewing the end of her pen, as she mulled over answers.

In ten minutes she'd completed the puzzle. He'd liked that about her, that she was sharp, and determined, and independent.

Too independent apparently. So independent she thought she didn't need him.

He was a PR expert, he knew all about making the best of a bad situation, of turning what might look like a disaster to a person's advantage.

He followed her glance to the clock. "Yeah, I think we can go now."

She smiled her relief and practically leaped from the bed, darting to the bathroom. Only for a moment did he let himself visualize the body he once knew so well, beneath the stream of the shower.

Max was stowing their bags in his car as Gillian stood talking with Laura in the marbled entry foyer hung with family portraits. She didn't understand why someone who was part of such a loving and close family would so assiduously avoid that kind of closeness for himself.

Unless it was just her he avoided it with.

Ethan sat happily on Laura's hip, studying with eyes and fingers the dangling necklace hanging at her throat.

Their time with his family this morning had been less awkward than Gillian had expected. But only a little. Laura and Stephen did their best to make her feel welcome but beneath their natural warmth she could see the questions and doubts in their eyes. She didn't blame them. Thankfully, Ethan provided a distraction that they all appreciated. She and Max had made their excuses and got ready to leave as soon as was polite.

Soon she'd be in the sanctuary of her own home. Back in her own territory. She held tight to the prospect. After the whirlwind of the past twenty-four hours, she only had to get through one and a half more before she'd have some space to collect her thoughts.

Laura looked about her then called, "Stephen. They're going." When Stephen failed to materialize, Laura touched a hand to Gillian's arm and said, "I'll be back in a minute, I'll just go find him." Carrying Ethan away as though she'd done it countless times before, she left Gillian alone.

She breathed in the blessed silence, her first few moments alone since she'd gotten into the car with Max yesterday. Home. Soon. She had no idea how things would go from here. But the worst was over. She'd married him. Even saying the fateful words *for better or for worse*. So, he had what he'd wanted, his name on a marriage certificate beside hers. Ethan had parents who were married. And for what it was worth, and for however long Max's interest lasted, she would be glad of it, would make the most of it.

Gillian crossed to the large family photo hanging amidst a cluster of individual portraits. She'd glimpsed the photos when she first came in yesterday but had had other things on her mind than stopping to inspect them.

The photo showed a young family beneath a spreading

autumnal oak. The shot wasn't formally posed, far from it, almost none of the laughing and numerous family members were looking directly at the camera. Almost too numerous. She studied the picture then counted the children, trying to identify each of them.

At the sound of footsteps on the tiled floor she glanced over her shoulder to see Max watching her, his expression remote, his arms folded across his chest. "The bags are in the car. Where's Ethan?"

"Your mom has him." She looked back at the photo.

Six children, not the five she knew about. Two of the boys, with their arms slung over each other's shoulders, identical except for their shirts. Two young Maxes. She was guessing around ten years old. And she was guessing one of them was the mysterious Dylan Carter had mentioned last night. A band tightened around her chest. A deep estrangement or death were the only explanations she could come up with for the fact that Max hadn't so much as mentioned him. And of those two, given the warmth of his family, death seemed the most likely. But when? How?

She turned back to Max, questions teeming in her mind. Now both his and his mother's reactions on learning Ethan's birthday made sense. But she read in his narrowed eyes and the arms folded across his chest, a warning to ask none of them. "I'll go find the others," was all he said as he left.

He'd had a twin.

And he wasn't going to say anything about it to her.

They pulled into her driveway, ending the silence of the trip. A silence filled with unspoken questions. She hadn't asked about his twin and he certainly hadn't raised the subject. Would he ever? Did she have any right to ask or to know? She couldn't come close to imagining how catastrophic losing a twin brother must have been for him. But the questions about

Max and his twin were in some ways just a mental diversion from the more pressing question of what now.

Max cut the engine but left his hands resting on the steering wheel. Too silent.

She looked at her house, her haven. Now she would get some respite from the previous day's—and night's—upheaval. Space. Freedom. Finally. For however long she could make it last.

There would be time to figure out next steps, to transition into their new arrangement. His urgency had abated from the time she'd married him.

Max helped her and Ethan inside and carried their bags upstairs. Gillian crouched in front of Ethan to remove the T-shirt he'd managed to spill water down the front of.

Gone. Soon Max would be gone. She held on to that thought as she blew a raspberry on her laughing son's tummy. Laughing in her turn. Soon she'd have the space to make sense of where her life was now at. So much had happened yesterday. It seemed a lifetime ago.

Max came lightly back down the stairs, his stride carrying him to the front door. Gillian held her breath. Ethan escaped her grasp and trotted to the living room, eager to play with his trains. Max paused with his hand on the handle. "I'll get my things and be back in an hour."

Seven

"Back here?" Gillian repeated, straightening from her crouch. "With what things?"

"I don't have much. Just my clothes and a few books. I lent my apartment back east to a friend and have been living at the Beach and Tennis Club."

"Your clothes." She sounded like a dim-witted echo, but she couldn't quite bring herself to accept what he was saying. "But…you're not…you don't think…?"

He frowned, opening the door to let in bright rays of winter sunshine. "We're married. So that my son can have two parents. So there won't be messy, part-time custody issues. Naturally we're going to live together. What did you think?"

Her mind and her heart raced. She certainly hadn't thought that. She deliberately hadn't thought anything at all. Shutting out the possibilities and probabilities. Because if she had allowed herself to think about it she would have known. A simple addition of two and two to get a solid four. Max and his determination. The way he wanted to order his world, and the people in it, to his liking.

But the prospect was too unnerving. Max in permanent close proximity. Where she could watch him, touch him, share things with him. Maybe want things from him. All bad.

"And here," he continued, oblivious to, or perhaps just unconcerned by, her spiraling agitation, "is far more suitable for a child than the Tennis Club. You have to see that. Ultimately, I'll buy another house for us or have one built. In fact, I noticed a for-sale sign on a beachfront property—"

"No." She shook her head.

"No?"

"We can't move. It would be too disruptive for Ethan. He's not even used to you yet."

"Fair enough." He looked around her simple home. A home that she knew was nothing like the mansions and luxury apartments that made up his world. But he seemed unperturbed by the differences.

And maybe she should be grateful for that fact. Maybe. But right now she couldn't find that emotion in her. She tried to formulate a quick and convincing argument that would stop Max from moving in, or at least put him off.

But words failed her. He watched her for several seconds and when still she didn't speak, said, "Good, that's settled then." And left.

Clutching Ethan's damp T-shirt to her chest, Gillian leaned against the nearest wall.

Disruptive?

For Ethan?

She pushed off from the wall. She had limits, but things had happened so fast the past two days that she hadn't had time to draw a line and hold to it.

That time had come.

She'd let him live here if that was what he thought he wanted. She'd even try to make the adjustment easy for him. For Ethan's sake. But if he thought anything else about this marriage—sex—was going to be real, he was very much mistaken. Or at least she wanted him to be.

He'd crushed her hopes and dreams once already. She wasn't going to let herself even have hopes and dreams again where he was concerned. That kind of relationship was both too much and not enough for where she was at now.

Already last night, in the darkness, she had wanted him. But she'd been caught unprepared. A weak moment. It wouldn't happen again. She couldn't let it.

True to his word he was back in an hour. He carried one suitcase and one bulging garment bag, holding the Italian tailor-made suits that always looked so good on him.

She opened the front door ready to set the ground rules.

"I'll need a key." He got in the first words.

He set his bags down and Gillian picked her keys out of the bowl on the nearby table and worked her key off the key ring. "Here. Now you can walk in and out of my home, my life, at will." She hadn't meant to let her bitterness, her fear show.

She turned but he stilled her with a hand on her arm, his grip firm, his blue gaze intense. "You're right about the walking in part. But not the walking out."

"You walked away from me before."

"Yes, but I'm not here for you, I'm here for Ethan."

Which she knew. And still the words felt like a blow. Putting her in her place. She'd do well to always remember that. *She* didn't matter to him.

"I don't walk away from my responsibilities."

"He's not just a responsibility. He's a little boy."

"He's *my* little boy."

"Our," she corrected him. If there were things she needed

to remember there were also things she couldn't let him forget.

He dropped his hand from her arm.

"And before you know it," she said, "before you've had time to decide whether this is truly what you want, he'll love you with all his heart. You'll hurt him, scar him if you leave." Like he'd hurt her. "He'll grow up blaming himself, thinking there's something wrong with him."

His eyes narrowed on her and a sudden yawning silence stretched. Finally, he spoke. "What aren't you telling me?"

"Nothing." Too astute, too perceptive he always was. Always cutting to the unseen heart of the matter.

"Who walked away from you?"

Gillian swallowed. Was she that transparent?

"We never talked about your parents."

"Just like we never talked about yours."

"But you've met mine now. You told Mom you didn't know your father." His voice was gentle, coaxing.

Hide it or get it out in the open? Hiding it only gave it power it didn't deserve. "My mother is wonderful. My father, on the other hand, couldn't decide whether he really wanted to be in our life. He came and went for months at a time, till finally when I was four he went and never came back." She was a grown woman but she could still feel her younger self's pain and confusion and blame. The feeling of inadequacy was something she'd had to battle hard. She would do anything to make sure Ethan never felt that.

Max regarded her awhile longer. A sympathy she didn't want softened his gaze. "I'm sorry." He touched his fingertips to her jaw. "And for what it's worth, it was his loss." The hand dropped away and the sympathy left his eyes. "But unlike your father, I have decided. I want in. And I'm not going, not today, not tomorrow, not until Ethan himself leaves home. I'm doing the right thing here."

It was everything she wanted to hear but didn't dare trust. "I know. Aren't you honorable. What if you find a way to decide that leaving is the honorable thing to do?"

He shook his head. "I'm not leaving. What's it going to take for you to believe that?"

"Weeks' and weeks' worth of disrupted sleep because he's sick or teething. You not reacting when milk gets spilled in the keyboard of the laptop you left open and out. You having to cancel social engagements because you can't find a sitter, having to give up Saturday golf because it takes up too much of your weekend. And all with no end in sight. Trading in your coupe for a car that's actually suitable for a child."

"I can do all of that, Gillian. I *want* to do all of that." He was so calm, so reasonable, making a mockery of her anxiety and her fears.

"We'll see."

"You doubt me?"

"Yes." He had no idea what he was getting into.

"Fair enough," he said. "Time will prove you wrong."

"It'll prove one of us wrong." She turned away from the steely determination in his eyes. "I only hope it's me. I'll show you the house."

"Gillian." He caught up to her on the lowest step and circled her wrist with his fingers.

Slowly, she turned to him.

"I didn't mean to hurt you. Three years ago. I was trying to save you hurt."

"You didn't hurt me," she lied. "We both knew what we had and didn't have." He released her wrist and she led the way to the bedrooms upstairs, Max close on her heels. "My room." She pointed to the first—firmly closed—door. She knew she'd need some kind of sanctuary in her home—her room was it.

Max lifted an eyebrow and a light glinted in his blue eyes.

"Is it locked, too? Are there weapons on the other side of it? The key to your chastity belt, perhaps?" Her lips twitched in response. He'd always been able to do that, make her see the funny side of a situation even when she was trying to be serious.

She'd liked him once precisely because he was honorable and he could make her laugh. And it hadn't hurt that the physical chemistry between them had been combustible. Such that it seemed a single glance from him would have had the power to laser through any chastity belt.

"Ethan's room." She pressed on, relaxing a little but still determined to show him that she was the one calling the shots here. She'd left that door open. Ethan's bed, with its dinosaur bedspread, and his bookcase and shelves of toys were visible. "There's only one bathroom up here. I'm not quite sure how that's going to work."

"We'll find a way. I'll fit around your schedule."

"How very accommodating of you."

Undaunted, he smiled at her sarcasm. Clearly, now that he'd gotten what he wanted, he was determined not to let her goad him. And if that was the case Gillian knew better than to fight it.

"Do you own this place or rent it?"

"I own it. I inherited it from my grandmother." The house was what had initially brought her to Vista del Mar. She couldn't have afforded a place this big and this close to the beach otherwise. But it was the job and the community she'd found here that kept her here. She even had Mrs. McDonald next door, who enjoyed babysitting Ethan whenever Gillian needed it, a substitute, she claimed, for her own grandchildren on the east coast.

"It has good bones."

"Long-term I'd like to renovate. But it's not a priority."

"Kristan would love to get her hands on it."

He'd mentioned that Kristan did up old houses for a living. It was on the tip of her tongue to ask more when she stopped herself. She had enough on her hands for the moment dealing with Max without bringing in extra family members.

Gillian pushed open the third door. "Your room." It shared a wall with hers. She stepped into the guest room dominated by a broad bed covered with a rich blue bedspread. With its heavy dresser and antique wall clock it was, she realized, a masculine room. As though it was waiting for Max to come and occupy it. The thought appalled her.

He followed her in and set his bag on the floor and laid his garment bag on the bed. He pulled open the doors of the wardrobe.

"I did my best to empty it in the time you were gone." She spoke to his back. "But that stuff on the shelves, old textbooks and boxes of paperwork, will take longer to sort through."

"Don't worry about it. We've got time." He pointed at his bags. "Besides, that's all I have." He crossed to the desk. She knew he saw and recognized the dictionary and thesaurus he'd once given her. To have removed them now would have been to admit that he still had some kind of power over her, that she gave consequence to his opinion. The books were useful, so she'd left them out.

"Where do you work if you're working from home?"

She nodded at the desk. "There, usually." The room had doubled as an office and a guest room. "I can work at the kitchen table easily enough."

"You have internet?"

"Yes."

"Wireless?"

"No."

"I'll sort it out."

It was on the tip of her tongue to refuse the offer. She disliked the contrary impulse, but she didn't want him thinking he could waltz in and reorganize her life. Although, that was, she admitted, pretty much what he'd done. What she'd let him do. It was too late to dig her toes in now, particularly over something that could only be of benefit to her. "Wireless would be good," she conceded.

A grin softened his face as though he knew something of her dilemmas. He crossed to the bed, testing it with a bounce. "Feels comfortable." He glanced at the vertical slats of the headboard. His grin faltered and he turned to her frowning. "Is this…?"

Gillian swallowed and nodded.

Max's eyes darkened. Yes. It was the bed she'd had when they'd been together before. The bed they'd slept on together, made love on together. She'd bought herself a new one after they parted but kept this as her spare.

For a moment the memories stretched between them.

Their relationship had come to such an abrupt end. One moment everything had been joyous and passion-filled. The next—nothing. There had been no bad times. So all her memories of him were good. Better than good.

Him sitting on that bed, looking at her like that, sudden hunger in his gaze, brought so many of them back.

The steady ticking of the clock was the only sound—reminding her that they couldn't turn back time.

Gillian backed away and Max slowly stood. What they'd had hadn't been enough. For him. Or maybe it had been too much. She didn't know.

He stepped closer. "We need to talk."

Gillian backed some more toward the door. "I don't think that's a good idea. In here," she qualified. Because yes, they'd need to talk. But she'd seen the look in his eyes and knew she needed to get away. He could so effortlessly confuse her.

"You sat beside me *in* bed just this morning." He interrupted her reluctance.

"I had no alternative. But that was the last time."

"Do you really think so?" He shook his head, not believing her assertion but no more pleased by the attraction that simmered than she was.

"Yes. You're here, for however long you can stick it—"

He closed the distance between them, his eyes serious. "A long time. When I make up my mind to do something, nothing, and no one, deters me."

"So you say. And that being the case, for however long it lasts, we'll have our own spaces. This is the only room you'll be sleeping in. And my room is the only one I'll be sleeping in." Though she knew thoughts of him would torment her while she was in bed alone. So close, but so much separating them.

"It frightens me, too, these things I feel for you. I don't want them." The admission, coming from the invulnerable Max, surprised her.

"I'm not frightened." Another lie. She was terrified. Of all sorts of things, of all the ways Max being here could be bad. Or good. She remembered their breakfast this morning. She remembered other breakfasts. And she was so confused that she wasn't sure which would be worse for her peace of mind, bad or good.

"Why don't you get settled in," she said, her hand on the door frame, trying to sound like an impartial host. "Ethan and I will have lunch soon. You're welcome to join us."

"Thank you, I will." He stood. So close. So close that she'd only have to lift a hand to touch him.

"About lunch today, how about a picnic on the beach?"

She forced her gaze to the window. Outside the sun shone in a clear blue sky; it would be cool out but they could dress for it. Gillian hesitated. "Ethan would like that."

"And you?"

Did he really care whether she would like it? "Yes, I'd like it, too." It would certainly be easier than being in the confined spaces of her home with him, his presence ambushing her, surrounding her. Him within touching distance.

"Gillian, there was a lot that was very right with what we had."

"It was superficial."

"That was all I wanted at the time. I thought it was all you wanted, too."

"And what do you want now, Max?"

He stiffened, then stepped past her and out the door. "To be a good father to my son. That's the only important thing. I want what's best for him and I don't want to miss out on his life, on the good or the bad."

"Then we both want the same thing and we can't afford to make it complicated and to mess it up."

Max carried Ethan, asleep on his shoulder, back into the house. He'd fallen fast asleep in the few minutes' drive back from the beach, and Max, oblivious to the sand from Ethan's feet through his car and now on his shirt, had unfastened the buckles of the car seat and extricated Ethan as competently as though he'd been doing it for years.

Together they walked up the stairs to Ethan's room, where Max lay his son gently down on the bed. Gillian placed his blanket close to her little boy's loosely curled hand. They stepped back and looked at him.

"Does he always sleep this soundly?"

"Usually. And the beach always tires him out." They'd spent over an hour exploring tide pools and collecting shells. It had felt so strange and yet so very right—the three of them together. And Ethan was, without a doubt, enjoying the male attention.

In complete contrast to Gillian. The male attention had her on edge. The brush of Max's hand across hers, the way his gaze locked and held on hers or lingered appreciatively on her legs.

He was being considerate, and thoughtful. He was being charming and it was disconcertingly seductive. After three years of coping on her own, to have the help, the attention of a man, to feel not just noticed but desirable in a man's eyes, was a potent sensation. Every touch, every glance, brought back to life an attraction that wouldn't be denied.

"I'm going to take a shower." She turned from his contemplative gaze. She had sand all through her hair from the beach. And she also needed an excuse to be away from him, somewhere where she wouldn't feel his presence.

But she'd been wrong about not being aware of his presence in her bathroom. A bottle of his cologne sat on the vanity. The old-fashioned razor and soap brush he liked to shave with stood beside it. His shampoo and conditioner sat alongside hers in the shower. And as she showered, the water sluicing over her body, she thought of him, thought of the predicament she now found herself in. Parenting with him. Sharing a house with him. Sleeping on the other side of a wall from him, night after night.

And she knew she was in trouble.

Eight

Rafe Cameron looked up from his computer screen as Max entered his office first thing Monday morning. "You sorted out the problem with the journalist from the *Seaside Gazette?*" Like him, his boss wasted no time on preliminaries. It was one of the reasons they worked so well together.

Max lowered himself into one of the leather chairs opposite Rafe's broad desk. "Gillian Mitchell. In a manner of speaking," he said.

"Go on."

"I married her. I thought you should know."

Rafe's brows rose as he contemplated Max. "Not you, too. Is there something in the water in this place?" For a moment Max didn't know what he meant. Then he remembered that Chase Larson, Rafe's stepbrother and money manager, had recently broken the news to Rafe that Emma Worth, daughter of the founder of the company Rafe was taking over, was carrying his baby. Shortly afterward the two had married in a quiet ceremony on the Worth estate.

Rafe leaned back in his chair. "I know I ask a lot of you, and you've always given the job your all. But that's a little drastic. Even for you."

"I didn't do it for the job. There's more to it than that."

"I'm glad to hear it." Rafe's phone rang. He glanced at the caller ID. "It's my dad. He's just back from China so I ought to take it."

Max stood. "I'll go."

Rafe shook his head. "No need. This won't take long. I'm seeing them tonight. And I want to know what happened with the reporter."

Max crossed to Rafe's window. Between tall palms, and beyond the red-tiled roofs of Vista del Mar, a distant view of the Pacific Ocean sparkled. He could even glimpse the Tennis Club, so recently his home, up on its bluff. He tried not to listen in on the conversation between Rafe and his father, Bob, a man Max had met on a couple of occasions, a man he liked and respected. Bob and Penny, his second wife, had been on an extended sightseeing trip to China.

And even though Max wasn't listening, it was impossible not to hear the changes in Rafe's voice. Over the course of a few minutes his tone went from interested inquiry, to puzzlement, to the careful neutrality that Rafe used to conceal his feelings.

The call ended and Rafe put his phone on the desk in front of him and frowned at it for several seconds. "That was odd."

"Something happen in China?"

"No. China exceeded all their expectations. It's this Worth Industries takeover. Dad got funny about it."

"I didn't think he took an active interest in what you did with the business."

"That's just it. He doesn't. Usually. But he's worried I'm out for revenge."

Max cleared his throat and Rafe grinned. "So, okay, maybe that particular worry is not without cause. But there's something else going on. He started talking about revenge doing more harm than good. All deep and philosophical. It just wasn't like him. Usually, if he has something to say he says it. Yet he was skirting around something then. I'm sure of it." Rafe shook his head and his brow cleared. "Back to you. You married our problem at the *Seaside Gazette*."

"Gillian."

"So you said. Where'd that come from? You've always maintained that the life of a bachelor suits you fine."

"It does. Did," he corrected. Being a bachelor had allowed him to live his life on the surface. A choice he'd been happy with. But now, with Gillian and Ethan, undertows of emotion tugged at him. Currents threatened to take control, to drag him deep. He thought of them constantly. He thought of *her* constantly.

Rafe watched him while he decided how much his boss needed to know. "I knew her once before."

Rafe nodded for him to continue.

"Turns out she had my son." He still wasn't used to saying the words *my son*. They were still a novelty, and a surprising source of pleasure and pride.

Rafe tilted his head. "You're sure of that?"

"Yes. So we got married."

"She wouldn't be the first woman to retrospectively pick the best possible candidate for a father."

A swift and unexpected surge of irritation heated his blood. "She's not like that." It was okay for him to be angry at Gillian, to question her actions, but for some reason he didn't want anyone else doing it, especially someone who didn't even know her. "Besides," he added, "he looks just like me."

Rafe shrugged. "I guess that at least means she'll do what you say now."

Max thought of Gillian, strong-willed and determined. "I don't think it's going to be quite that simple." Rafe definitely didn't have any idea what she was like if he thought that was how it was going to work. "She's not exactly the sort to do what anyone else tells her." Not his Gillian. She was too independent for that. And she wasn't, he corrected himself, *his* Gillian. Yes, they were married but it was for Ethan's sake, and for Max's benefit in being a father to his son. But there was no *us* or *we* or *his*. Not emotionally. Not when it came to Gillian.

Physically there would be. Soon. He was giving her a little time to get used to the idea, to accept that the chemistry still simmered, that there was no point in denying it.

"I'm sure you'll manage it," Rafe said.

Max stood to leave. Out in the hallway he passed Chase heading for Rafe's office. The man had an almost dreamy expression on his face.

As Max settled into his office chair his thoughts swerved to Gillian. They'd had dinner together as a family last night. The three of them at Gillian's small wooden table. Thank goodness his son had kept up a stream of chatter, even if much of it was unintelligible.

If anyone had asked him, even just a couple of days ago, how he'd feel about such a meal, he'd have said there was nothing he'd like less. The reality had been a blessed contrast to the solitary meals which, through his own choice, he ate so many nights over work.

He'd shared moments with both his wife and his son, glances, touches, laughter. It was a whole new world. But one he couldn't afford to be beguiled by. He was here to be part of their lives and for his son, and by default Gillian, to be a part of his life.

But not his heart. He couldn't afford for them to lay claim to his heart.

He knew she'd seen the photo with Dylan in it. And he could only be thankful she'd asked no questions, even though he'd seen them in her eyes. She was a journalist, it was in her nature to be inquisitive, but that was one area she'd get no access. That was private. The death of his twin had scarred him so deeply that it overshadowed his life from that point on. Nothing ever touching him so deeply again, not grief, and not joy.

He didn't have it in him to bond so closely with anyone again. He never even wanted to have it in him.

Which meant he had to set boundaries for himself. He would go home tonight, help with Ethan's mealtime and bath time and bedtime, allow himself the simple pleasure of reading a story to his son, of feeling his little arms snake around his neck as he hugged him good-night, and then he would go out for dinner. On his own. He could come back to the office and work. He would set the pattern for how this arrangement with Gillian was going to work.

As he pulled into her driveway that evening he told himself it wasn't anticipation he felt quickening within him. And if it was, it could only be for the novelty of seeing his son who'd accepted him so quickly, so unconditionally.

The anticipation was nothing to do with seeing Gillian—who'd accepted him into her life only because she had no choice and whose acceptance came fortified with conditions and parameters.

She was defensive and reserved—except when she forgot to be.

He loosened his tie as he walked toward the house, his laptop case in one hand. He'd last seen her this morning dressed in a sleek, sexy skirt and white blouse as she'd leaned into her car to buckle Ethan into his seat. It was an image that had presented itself in his mind far too many times today—the curve of waist and hip, shapely calves, slender ankles, all perfectly designed to stir lust. A purely evolutionary reaction.

She'd glanced over her shoulder and caught him watching, and for an instant she'd seen the physical awareness in his eyes and responded; heat had arced between them. But by the time she straightened, all trace of heat was gone—replaced by careful neutrality. He'd feigned interest in an email on his phone and she'd folded her arms across her chest as she briskly explained their routine to him—that she'd take Ethan to the local preschool where he would spend the morning while Gillian worked, before picking him up soon after his lunchtime and coming home to work the second part of her day. She fit her hours around his afternoon nap and worked most evenings as well.

It didn't sound like much of a life for her.

But when he thought about it, and tried to look at it objectively, neither did the life he'd carved for himself. Working all hours of the day, most evenings, most weekends, breaking to play tennis or work out at the gym, socializing with the "right" people, colleagues and associates, friends with political clout and connections within the media. And he'd dated—beautiful, available, shallow women. He vacationed twice a year—a winter holiday on the ski fields of Switzerland, summer in the Caribbean, always staying at exclusive resorts, dining in fine restaurants.

Never before had he spent two hours on the beach exploring rock pools and collecting shells. The concept had stirred a quiet voice to whisper that perhaps his outwardly successful life could be perceived as a little sterile, a little empty. He'd quashed the thought.

He turned his key in the front door. And despite the key, felt like an intruder, or at the least an imposter, as though he was stepping into someone else's life.

The babble of his son's chatter coming from the kitchen

drew him inside. He stopped in the doorway and watched. His son. His wife. The concept was surreal.

Ethan sat on a booster seat at the table eating a banana. At least Max thought he was supposed to be eating it, hard to be certain when much of the banana appeared to be squeezed between his fingers. Peas littered the floor around Ethan's chair.

Gillian, a rust-colored T-shirt clinging to her curves, her hair pulled back into a ponytail, looked up from her seat beside Ethan and saw him watching. And something in his expression made her smile, her lips tilting upward with suppressed laughter.

"Is that a laughing with me or at me smile?"

"At, definitely. You should see your face." Her eyes danced with merriment. Gillian was the only woman who'd ever laughed at him. Most took him as seriously as he took himself. It was provoking. It was refreshing. It made him want to retaliate, to turn the tables.

If he strode over and covered those smiling lips with his own, as he suddenly wanted to, she wouldn't be laughing.

"Daddy." Ethan lifted his banana-covered hands toward Max. He wanted Max to pick him up?

And this time Gillian laughed out loud. She had a throaty, sexy laugh. Once again she was laughing at him.

So he followed impulse, crossed the kitchen and as her smile dimmed and a wary light replaced the amusement in her eyes, he kissed her. His lips to hers, somewhere between gentle and demanding. He felt her shock, felt her momentary softening and savoring, felt the shared impulsive moment of need and desire. Her mouth was warm and pliable beneath his. She joined perfectly with him, making him want to stay here and absorb the pleasure of being with her just like this.

He straightened, and then, not meeting her gaze, turned and

planted a kiss on his son's head. "I'll just change and come back down, tiger." He spoke to Ethan then left the room.

It wasn't supposed to have been like that. The kiss had been to disconcert her, not him. He wasn't supposed to have reveled in the sensations.

Control. He was all about control. Of himself, of the situations he let himself get into. And it was time to re-establish it here. It was supposed to be her asking him to touch her, not the other way around.

He'd come back down, spend time with Ethan and then leave. Proving to himself and her that he was indifferent to the heat, remembered and present, between them.

Fifteen minutes later, Gillian listened for Max's tread on the stairs, her nerves on high alert. She sat cross-legged on the floor in front of the train set as Ethan hooked two carriages together.

Kissing hadn't been part of their deal. She'd wanted to kick herself. She knew she'd revealed too much in that brief kiss. He'd caught her unprepared and want had surfaced before she'd even thought to repress it. He'd always kissed like a dream, coaxing, giving, asking. A few seconds. That was as long as the kiss had lasted.

Too long for a kiss that should never have happened. And too short, clamored the part of her that ignored reason. The part of her that had been alone for too long. The part of her that had missed him and the potential of what they could have had from the very day he walked out of her life.

"If you've got things you want to do, I can play with him." Max stood in the doorway wearing faded, snug-fitting jeans, a black T-shirt stretching across his chest, and with eyes that saw too much.

"Thanks." Gillian scrambled to her feet. As they swapped positions their gazes locked, awareness passing between them.

The memory of his mouth on hers, the taste of him, the feel of him. The relentless tug of attraction. Did he feel it in the same way she did? Would he kiss her again, now?

Her body heating, she hurried from the room and set her laptop up on the kitchen table and tried to work. True to his word Max already had wireless set up for them. Just as, with her permission, he'd also engaged a housekeeping service, not wanting his presence to create extra work for her. She stared at the screen of her computer, supposedly working on the opening sentence for her next article. Half an hour later, she was still staring at the same blank screen. Still fighting the recollections and her reactions. Pathetic. Undisciplined. What was happening to her?

She knew the answer. Max.

She had to grow up and harden up.

Forcing herself to concentrate, she opened up a draft article on the outcome of the latest town hall meeting, the bulk of which had been given over to Rafe Cameron's takeover of Worth Industries. The piece was scheduled for a week's time. It was all but completed but she decided, as she leaned back in her chair, what she really needed was some information from Rafe. She wanted his side of the story. He'd so far ignored her requests for an interview. She could ask Max, but as with their previous relationship they hadn't discussed work. They had a tacit understanding that things were fraught enough between them as it was, without bringing their conflicting work agendas into the picture.

Ten minutes later she gave up the pretense of working and opted for a video game. One where she was a gun-toting heroine and could blast away anything and anyone who got in her way. A world where everything was simple. It was clear who were the good guys and who were the bad. And it stopped her thinking about Max.

Max who had left her. Max who was back in her life.

Max who kissed like a dream. Max who shared some of her thoughts about resuming the physical relationship between them. Physical but nothing more. Max who wouldn't share anything of himself. Nothing personal like the fact that he'd had a twin who had died.

A blast from a rocket launcher and the bad guys got her. She'd been less than halfway to her high score but far too distracted.

The internet was at her fingertips. It wouldn't be difficult to find out what had happened to Dylan. But she didn't want to pry. And she wanted Max to tell her himself. When he was ready. If he ever was. Was that too much to ask for?

And she wanted to know things the internet could never tell her, like how it had impacted him, how he'd survived.

She restarted her game and tried to shut out the sound of laughter from the family room, a mix of childish delight and masculine amusement.

"You still play that one?" Gillian's avatar went up in a ball of flames as she fumbled the keys. Even though she'd been busted, she shut the screen down. Max stood in the doorway, Ethan sitting in the crook of his arm.

She shrugged. "Sometimes."

"Looks like you're well set up for gaming in the family room, too."

"It shows that I don't get out a lot, huh." Gillian tried to make light of it. But what she really remembered was how she and Max used to play those games together. They were both fiercely competitive, whether it was racing cars around a track or through city streets, or hunting each other down through a futuristic city. They'd often bet on the outcome, the winner choosing how the other would reward them for their victory.

Usually that worked out well for both of them.

Needing to divert her attention, she glanced at her watch.

Get 2 Books FREE!

Silhouette® Books,
publisher of women's fiction,
presents

GET 2 BOOKS

We'd like to send you two *Silhouette Desire*® novels absolutely free.
Accepting them puts you under no obligation to purchase any more books.

HOW TO GET YOUR
2 FREE BOOKS AND 2 FREE GIFTS

1. Return the reply card today, and we'll send you two *Silhouette Desire* novels, absolutely free! We'll even pay the postage!

2. Accepting free books places you under no obligation to buy anything, ever. Whatever you decide, the free books and gifts are yours to keep, free!

3. We hope that after receiving your free books you'll want to remain a subscriber, but the choice is yours—to continue or cancel, any time at all!

EXTRA BONUS

You'll also get two free mystery gifts! (worth about $10)

FREE!

Return this card today to get
2 FREE BOOKS and 2 FREE GIFTS!

YES! Please send me 2 FREE *Silhouette Desire®*
novels, and 2 free mystery gifts as well. I understand
I am under no obligation to purchase anything, as
explained on the back of this insert.

*About how many NEW paperback fiction books have
you purchased in the past 3 months?*

❏ 0-2
E9UD

❏ 3-6
E9UP

❏ 7 or more
E9UZ

225/326 SDL

FIRST NAME	LAST NAME

ADDRESS

APT.#	CITY

STATE/PROV.	ZIP/POSTAL CODE

Visit us at:
www.ReaderService.com

▲ DETACH AND MAIL CARD TODAY! ▼

(S-D-03/11)

If offer card is missing, write to The Reader Service, P.O. Box 1867, Buffalo, NY 14240-1867 or visit www.ReaderService.com

BUSINESS REPLY MAIL

FIRST-CLASS MAIL   PERMIT NO. 717   BUFFALO, NY

POSTAGE WILL BE PAID BY ADDRESSEE

THE READER SERVICE
PO BOX 1867
BUFFALO NY 14240-9952

NO POSTAGE
NECESSARY
IF MAILED
IN THE
UNITED STATES

"Bath time, huh?" she said brightly. "Let's get you upstairs and undressed."

Max quirked an eyebrow.

"Not you—Ethan." Too late. Triggered by the recollections of one particular wager she'd lost, images of bathing Max flashed into her mind—lathering his broad muscled torso with soap, her hands sliding over slick skin.

"Do you want me to help?" Max asked, seemingly unaware.

"No. I'll be fine." Annoyed with herself, the words came out sharper than she'd intended.

"I'd like to," he said quietly, unperturbed. And it sounded like an order rather than an offer.

Gillian swallowed. "Sure."

Max carried Ethan up the stairs, leaving Gillian to follow.

They bathed Ethan, put him to bed, reading to him till his eyes drifted closed. And for a time they sat in silence, Gillian on the edge of the bed, Max perched on the small chair in Ethan's room, his elbows resting on his knees. Silence and awareness surrounded them.

What now? she wondered. Evenings with Ethan were structured, relatively predictable and easy. Evenings with Max, in this new situation, were an entirely unknown quantity. Time together. Just the two of them.

Max stood, his gaze steady on her. "I'm going out. I'll see you in the morning."

"Of course," she said, covering a surprise that she had no right to. He was here for Ethan alone. He had a life to live. One that she wasn't a part of, one that she knew nothing about. Unless she asked him to stay. To touch her. She opened her mouth but the words of surrender lodged in her throat.

She was still sitting watching Ethan sleep when her front door opened and shut.

And it was late that night as she lay in bed that she heard

him return. The soft noises of him getting ready for bed sounded through the wall. She imagined him climbing into the bed they'd once shared—back when everything between them had been simple.

Did he think of her? Sometimes she could swear the answer was yes.

Reaching above her head, she touched her fingertips to the wall that separated them.

Thoughts and midnight fantasies were making a mockery of her resolution not to be the one to give in. Fantasies about leaving her bed, going to the one they had once shared so enthusiastically, slipping beneath the sheets, pressing her body to his. It was as if invisible threads bound her to him. A new one twining with the others with every look, every accidental touch, pulling her inexorably toward him.

What would he do if she gave in to that pull?

He'd let her in. He'd even give her pleasure. He just wouldn't give her anything of himself, wouldn't let her touch his heart.

Not that she wanted to. Did she? Somewhere beneath the physical yearning for him was a deeper yearning.

And she so wasn't going there.

At midday on Thursday, Gillian stood in front of the reception desk at Cameron Enterprises trying to convince the beautiful but unobliging woman who manned it that she should be allowed through to put a few questions to Rafe. She was running out of time to include his side of the story in her article. Sometimes the personal, and ever so slightly pushy, approach worked best. She wasn't having much joy with it today. The receptionist wouldn't even confirm whether Rafe was in.

Max would answer her questions, but she didn't want Max's

smooth interpretations. She wanted to hear Rafe's words, watch Rafe's eyes.

"Gillian?" She turned at the sound of Max's voice and the surprise in it. "Is everything all right? Is Ethan okay?" Concern etched lines in his forehead.

"Everything's fine. Ethan's with Mrs. McDonald."

His gaze softened, and he raked a hand through his hair. Not, she was guessing, for the first time today. It was something he did when he worked. It served only to change him from suave and sexy to rumpled and sexy.

She realized she was staring. Drinking in the sight of him.

And he was staring back, his gaze lingering as though captivated.

The receptionist cleared her throat. "Ms. Mitchell wants to speak to Mr. Cameron."

Grasping her elbow with one hand, Max gestured with his other toward the suite of offices he'd just appeared from. "Ms. Mitchell," he said with pointed meaning, "can talk to me."

Nine

"Do they know we're married?" Gillian asked as he pushed open the door to his office. *That we've been living together? Do they know that you made my coffee this morning? That the scent of your aftershave lingers in my bathroom?*

He held the door as she walked past him. "Rafe knows. That's all. And he's not one for watercooler gossip."

Was there any significance to his lack of sharing that news? Did he not want people to know because he didn't consider it a real marriage? But given that she'd told no one either she decided not to probe too deeply for meaning.

"How did he take the news? First Chase and now you with connections to the opposition."

"If you want to know the truth, he thought that us being married would put you in his camp."

She spun back to him and caught the amusement in his eyes, the suppressed grin.

Gillian smiled. It was one of those increasingly frequent

moments of connection that, as always, hovered on the brink of something else, something that begged to be more. She dragged her thoughts back from the paths they wanted to run down. Paths that broke through restraint. "So he's not as smart as everyone says."

"Maybe not about relationships."

Any smugness Gillian might have felt vanished. Turned out she wasn't so smart about relationships either. It was there in his eyes, the wanting. It spoke to her without words, called to her.

She looked away from Max and around his office. A broad pale desk, clear except for his laptop and a coffee cup, dominated the center of the room; behind it rose a high-backed leather chair. A slender potted palm graced one corner of the room.

"So, is this business or—"

She swung back to him. The unspoken work hung in the air.

He still stood with his back to the door, but he was frowning as though he hadn't meant to further raise the spectre of pleasure. Something shifted in the air. Heat slithered down her spine. And suddenly it grew difficult to breath. The cool reserve of the man sharing her house had vanished. Memories of forbidden kisses surfaced. Kisses that had led nowhere because of where they were at the time, because of Ethan's presence.

"Business." Gillian swallowed. That was why she'd come here, but her thoughts were anything but businesslike. This was the first time she'd been alone with him and away from Ethan, away from the home they both trod so warily in.

She had to look away; she couldn't let him see her need for him. She crossed to the tinted windows and stared out unseeing. "I wanted to ask Rafe some questions."

"Perhaps I can help."

He *could* help. Only he could.

But right now they couldn't get any farther apart. He with his back to the door, she across the office at the window. The distance felt like a canyon. She ached to cross it and didn't know how, didn't know the right steps to take. The ones that would stop her falling into the abyss. The click of the door locking sounded in the stillness.

"Gillian." Her name was a whisper threaded with need. Close.

He stood at her side. Canyon crossed.

Like Dorothy in *The Wizard of Oz,* the power, the words she needed to say were inside her, had been all along. "Max." She reached blindly for him.

His palms slid over her jaw, fingers threading into her hair as his lips covered hers, searching and hungry. As hungry as she was for him, a wanting she'd denied since he'd stormed back into her life, a wanting she'd denied for three lonely years.

A wanting that grew more powerful, more urgent as his mouth moved over hers. In this unrestrained kiss, one that was proving no point other than that she could lose herself in him, she remembered everything. The promise and fulfillment of him.

She held on to him, gripping his shoulders even as she was gripped by sensation in return. His lips on hers, his arms around her, their bodies melding together.

This was what she had been missing. The lack of him had been the empty space within her.

She found buttons, undid them and slid her hands beneath his shirt over the hard plane of his stomach, up over his chest. Beneath her palm, his heart beat as wildly as hers. His breathing had become as ragged as hers. His need for her inflamed her own.

She wanted him.

Desperately.

The needs so long denied were beyond repressing now.

She wanted everything he could offer. And he would know it.

Just as she'd worked his buttons undone, he'd found hers and returned the favor. With one arm around her, holding her to him, his other hand found and caressed her breast, cupping the weight, teasing the aching nipple so that she jerked with the need that streaked through her and gasped into his mouth.

In their kissing they turned and moved as though in a dance till she felt his desk press against the backs of her legs. He lifted her up, setting her on his desk. He pushed up what little of her skirt hadn't already ridden up. His palms spread over her thighs and slid upward as he stepped into the space between her legs.

He uttered a gentle oath under his breath as his fingers rose to trace the edge of her bra over the swell of her breasts, and his thumbs rubbed over the peaks of her nipples.

Dipping his head, he claimed a nipple through delicate lace, sucking, creating a gentle abrasion. She bit her lip to keep from crying out as sensation, a jolt of current, coursed through her.

She was so lost in swirling feeling she didn't realize he'd unfastened the clasp between her breasts till her bra fell open. She heard his harshly indrawn breath, saw the wonder and desire in his eyes. Wonder and desire that made her burn even more for him.

He bent his head and nipped gently at the spot where her shoulder swept to her neck. She tipped her head back, gave him access to her throat, heedless of everything except the heat he ignited, the fire within her. In scant minutes he'd turned her to a quivering mass of need.

With his hands hot and possessive on her breasts, he trailed kisses up her neck, igniting fire across her skin. He worked his way along her jaw till his lips found hers and his fingers threaded into her hair, angling her head to deepen the kiss. His tongue teased hers, skimmed teeth. Her mouth, her body, remembered and responded to him. He was her past and her present. Her now. Sensing and responding to her needs. Taut with needs of his own.

He stepped back long enough to ease her panties from her, dropping them to the floor before stepping close again.

She slid her palms over his chest, over small male nipples, over contoured muscle, over the gentle abrasion of hair. She remembered his touch, remembered the feel of him beneath her fingers, and remembered the desperate wanting he stirred, the tingling that crawled through her. A wanting that had only intensified in the years she'd been without him.

Her hands dipped eagerly lower to unfasten his pants and free the length of him. He produced a condom that they put on him together. Wrapping her fingers around the heavy, solid silk of him, she guided him toward her center. She rubbed him against herself, positioned him perfectly. Then looked up. He watched her from hooded eyes, his lips parted, his breathing heavy.

"Touch me," she whispered as she wrapped her legs around his hips. "Take me." Her voice was desperate with wanting.

With a savage groan, he slid home in a single slow deep thrust, burying himself in her. Filling her.

Time stood still, poised on the brink of perfection.

He slid slowly out and back again, his fingers pressing into her skin as he gripped her hips to pull her on him even more fully.

And then again and again.

Every touch, every movement, drove her need higher till she was lost in a fog of desperation that built and built along with the fierce rhythm they found until she exploded around him, fighting back the scream that clawed at her throat.

He plunged his fingers into her hair as he covered her mouth with his, taking her cry of pleasure inside him as she clutched at his shoulders, her anchor in a spinning world, as his release pulsed inside her, his hips driving his final thrusts against hers.

Satisfaction rippled through her as the tension seeped from their bodies. Muscles relaxing, he wound his arms around her, held her tight to him, his head resting on hers. Gillian inhaled the scent of him—cologne, man, sex. She wanted to stay like this. The one place things were pure and simple between them.

He tilted her face up, studied her for a moment, then brushed a gentle kiss across her lips.

Too soon he pulled away from her, rebuttoning his shirt, refastening his pants. Her head forward, her hair curtaining her face, Gillian fumbled the catch of her bra. Strong hands eased hers aside, capable, steady fingers did the clasp up. She met his gaze as he trailed his fingertips over the swell of her breasts before reaching for the sides of her blouse and reverently buttoning up the buttons he'd so recently undone.

She could read little of his thoughts in his steady blue eyes. Could only hope nothing of hers showed. Lovemaking had always been seismic between them, but she didn't think it could be enough anymore. She wanted…more. That cry she'd swallowed had been his name. They never should have… She looked away, eased herself off his desk, found her panties and pulled them up her legs, smoothed her skirt back into place. Had they just destroyed the fragile balance of their arrangement, of their developing relationship?

Max watched Gillian shutting herself off from him. He touched her chin, felt her new tension, a fear almost. With gentle pressure he lifted her face so she had to meet his gaze. "It's okay."

She gave a tiny shake of her head. "Is it?"

On some level, he'd known almost from the start that their physical relationship would resume, though it had taken a little longer to acknowledge that fact and, till today, to yield the desire. What he hadn't known was that giving in and making love to Gillian would shake the careful foundations of his world.

"Don't make it complicated. Don't get all regretful." Easy for him to say because he was making the same heartfelt pleas to himself. If they could just keep this simple. He never deluded himself, but he was giving it his best shot now.

"But…"

He shook his head. "You know we're good together, in so many ways. And this is most definitely one of them. Don't make it confusing or something dark and furtive. We can have this much."

"But…" That same word again, an unfinished protest.

He waited and, when she said nothing more, prompted. "But what?"

She opened her mouth, the lips he'd so recently kissed now devoid of lipstick, looking kiss-swollen and temptingly kissable again. Her hair, disordered and wild around her face. She looked exactly like she was, a woman who'd just had sex with him in his office. "Nothing," she said with a frown, the word clipped.

"Tell me what's on your mind."

"It's just that…"

He waited.

"This—" she gestured between the two of them "—could complicate everything."

"Or it could simplify everything."

"I don't think that's how it works."

"How about we try it and see?"

A one-sided grin touched her lips. He knew that half smile, her cynical reporter's grin. "So you get sex on tap?"

Sex on tap with Gillian sounded like his own personal fantasy. "Not just me. You can't tell me I was the only one who wanted that. That I'm the only one of us thinking about when and where it's going to happen next."

She picked up her purse. "I'm not ready for this conversation."

"It's not like you to run."

"This is not like any situation I've been in before. I need time to think. It's not just the two of us to consider. We can't walk away if it goes bad. We're married now."

He nodded. It wasn't like any situation he'd been in before either. Though he didn't feel the need to think about it. "We could analyze this to death or we could just accept it for what it is. Great, almost perfect chemistry. And we could let it go at that without the need to probe it from fifty different angles, to look for possible pitfalls."

She headed for his door. "Maybe it is that simple. For you. But I just need to be certain. Everything has happened so fast between us. Including this." Confusion clouded her green eyes. Gillian who always had a clear-cut position on everything, Gillian who always knew where she stood, and had no qualms letting everyone else know.

She stopped with her hand on his door, seemed to be gathering her strength, putting on her facing-the-world attitude. "Wait," he said.

He crossed to her and did his best to smooth her hair back into place. She bit her lip and wry amusement touched her eyes. "Do I look like…?"

He nodded.

"Damn."

"Take a minute. At least till that flush of color fades from your cheeks, and from here." He touched the vee of skin revealed by her blouse, but only briefly.

Gillian swallowed.

He kissed her once quickly, lightly, because he could. Because after days of restraint, having broken through that barrier, something within him sang in celebration.

Then he stepped back from the temptation of her. "These questions you had for Rafe—you can ask me."

She shrugged then glanced at his door, clearly torn between her need to leave and to not be seen looking like a woman who'd just had sex with him in his office. "I wish I could but it's more personal opinion and background that I'm after."

She took a deep breath and pulled open his door. Max walked with her through to the reception area.

Her step faltered when she saw Maggie Cole, one of the secretaries, handing a sheaf of papers to the receptionist. Maggie looked over, her gaze taking in Max's hand at Gillian's elbow, her eyes behind the lenses of her glasses widening. "Gillian," she said, surprise in the questioning pitch to her voice.

Gillian shook her head. "I'll catch you later."

"We're still on for coffee?" Maggie asked.

"Absolutely," Gillian said a little too brightly before turning for the door.

Max hadn't realized the two women knew each other. But given Maggie's surprise, it didn't look as though Gillian had told her anything about their marriage.

He opened the exit door for her and when she would have walked past him without stopping, put a hand on her shoulder, and waited till she turned to him. "I'll see you tonight."

Her gaze dipped to his lips and a small secret smile played about her mouth as she nodded.

Ten

"You look tired." Gillian looked up to see Max standing in the bathroom doorway watching her.

She straightened. She'd been leaning on the edge of the bath, her fingers trailing in the water as Ethan played. It wasn't surprising that she might look tired considering the turn their relationship had taken. Since that day in his office over a week ago their nights had become a time of shared passion.

"You really know how to make a gal feel good." She said it blithely, pretended she was indifferent to his thoughts of her. But he was right. She was tired.

His gaze stayed steady on her, blue and intense.

Weariness vanished as sensation skittered down her spine. No matter how tired she might be he had that same effect on her. "Have you eaten?" he asked.

"Not yet. I was going to fix myself some dinner after I put Ethan to bed."

He watched her for long moments till, uncomfortable under

his scrutiny, she turned back to Ethan. "Bath time's over, buddy. Pull the plug and stand up."

Max materialized beside her holding a towel. As the water drained from the bath, Ethan stood and held his arms up to his father. Such simple trusting, no second-guessing, no wondering.

Max had left a message on her phone saying he wouldn't be home in time for Ethan's dinner. As her son had eaten she'd tried to be grateful that she didn't have the confusion of Max's presence, didn't have to hide anything of herself. But like her son, who'd asked for Daddy, she knew that an intransigent, insensible part of her missed him.

Just for the adult company, she told herself, knowing it was a lie.

They did things together at home. Some as a family but many, many things where it was just the two of them. But apart from that one time in his office she didn't see him outside of home. They'd never been out in public together. And even within their home he kept so much of himself from her still.

She knew his family had called asking to see them again, but she'd heard him on the phone making their excuses, putting them off to some unspecified date. He'd yet to mention Dylan to her.

As Max lifted Ethan from the bath, she stood. Max's gaze dipped to her chest. Her T-shirt clung damply to her breasts. His Adam's apple slid as he swallowed and then turned away.

They were tucking Ethan into bed when there was a knock at the door. "I'll get it," Max said as he left the room.

Ten minutes later Gillian followed the sound of voices downstairs to find Max and Mrs. McDonald engrossed in conversation.

Mrs. McDonald practically beamed at her. It appeared even her elderly neighbor wasn't immune to the appeal of Max. "It's well past time you had an evening out. It's been far too long. And so nice of your young man to arrange it. It's about time you had someone looking out for you."

"An evening out?" She looked from her neighbor to Max.

"Yes," he said. "Let's go."

"Where? I'm not ready to go anywhere. Look at me."

And so he did, and she wished she could retract the command because his gaze on her always elicited a response. "Maybe a jacket, it'll be cool out. But other than that you are ready. Trust me."

Outside, he reached for her hand, wrapping his fingers around hers.

That simple touch felt so natural. So good.

"Where are we going? What have you got planned?" She knew he wasn't planning what her undisciplined mind had leaped to as soon as she asked the question.

He smiled. "Trust me."

Trust was such a loaded word between them, Gillian made no response.

He drove to the ocean. Once there, he pulled a blanket and a hamper from the trunk and carried them down to the beach, spreading the blanket out and inviting her to sit. The sun had already set but the sky was still light though quickly fading. He poured a glass of wine and handed it to her.

Pleasure and ease stole through her as waves washed to the pebbled beach and she sipped the light fruity sauvignon blanc.

Later, when he topped up her glass unasked, she turned to him. "What's this about, Max?"

"This is about you," he said after a pause.

"About me?"

"You looked tired. And tense. And I wanted to do something for you. I didn't know if you'd let me take you away somewhere, but I figured this would be okay."

She wanted to argue, to tell him he was wrong. But he wasn't. He was so right and it was unsettling to think that he'd both noticed and chosen to do something about it. Underneath the no-nonsense exterior lay something softer, someone who thought of others. "Thank you," she finally said. "This is lovely."

He handed her a plate of food, prepared, she assumed because of the array of delicacies, by one of the more expensive local restaurants.

She didn't want to need him, or rely on him, or even enjoy his company too much. The kind of one-sided attachment that went beyond the physical that could only lead to hurt.

"Now, eat and drink and relax."

It was surprisingly easy to follow his suggestion, a relief almost. Thoughts of her situation ebbed away till all that was left was the dwindling evening and her ever-present awareness of Max as he leaned back on his elbows, his legs stretched in front of him, his gaze trained out to sea.

When they'd eaten, they walked along the beach. Once again he took her hand. Once again she was far too aware of the touch, that tentative connection.

As the first stars came out they turned back for the car. "Are you going to tell me about Dylan?"

His grip tightened around her hand. They walked on several more steps. "No. Not now."

She got the feeling he meant not ever.

Gillian stopped. "I think it's important."

"It's not something I want to talk about."

"But—"

He pulled her into his arms and kissed her, covered her lips with his to seal away the words she'd been going to say. It was no more than a diversionary tactic and she knew better than to be diverted by it.

She knew better. But the heat of him overpowered the weak

voice of reason. The sensation of his lips on hers stole words and breath. His hands around her shoulders pulled her into a world where it was just her and him.

His mouth moved over hers, at once seeking and giving. Tongues twined in an erotically familiar dance.

She almost wept with the wanting of him. Only him.

He knew how she liked to be kissed, knew precisely how she liked to be held and touched. His palm was warm against the curve of her waist, warmer as it slid upward beneath her T-shirt, hot as it cupped the shape and weight of her breast, his thumb roving over hardening nipples, sending shards of heat arrowing through her. Intense. Sudden. Needy.

Her hips rocked against his as her hands slid beneath the soft skin-warmed cotton of his shirt and found greater warmth in the strong contours of his back.

He kissed her in the moonlight and when he was kissing her, nothing else mattered. Everything was perfect in her world. And building to an even greater perfection.

For the longest time they stood locked together on the beach. And had it not been for that very fact—that they were in the middle of a public though deserted beach—that kiss would have led to so much more.

It was Max who ended it, lifting his head, and for just a moment holding her to him, his arms locked behind her, as though she meant something to him, before dropping his hand to hers and leading her back to the car.

"Earth to Gillian."

Gillian stopped the slow stirring of her coffee and looked up. Maggie sat opposite, watching her, curiosity in her gaze.

She and Maggie had a semiregular coffee date here at the Bistro by the Sea, using the time to catch up on each other's news or plan a movie evening. Today they sat outside enjoying the mild spring sunshine.

"Where were you?"

They were close but not close enough that Gillian could tell her friend that she'd mentally been back in Max's office, on his desk. She wasn't *that* close to anyone. Seeing Maggie for the first time since that day at Cameron Enterprises had brought it back to the forefront of her mind.

"I was thinking about work stuff." It was a stretch, but she *had* gone to Max's office that day with the intention of discussing work. Even if she'd ended up half-naked on his desk.

A gentle breeze blew in from the sea and Maggie touched her fingers to the bun at the back of her head, checking it was still neatly contained. "And here was me," she said sweetly, "thinking it might be the fact that you got married without so much as telling me, that was occupying your thoughts."

Gillian set her spoon down. "Did Max say?"

"Max?" Maggie squawked. "You married Max Preston? That's why you were with him the other day."

She grimaced. "I guess that means he didn't say."

Maggie shook her head emphatically.

"Then how did you know?"

"Your ring." Maggie nodded at Gillian's left hand resting on the table.

"Oh." Gillian slipped her hand to her lap. "It was kind of a hasty decision."

"Obviously, given that last time we talked about relationships you refused to so much as even consider the possibility of dating. You were too busy, you said. You didn't have time or space in your life."

"It's a long story."

Maggie watched her closely.

"And I will tell you. Soon. I'm just not ready to talk about it yet, it's too…"

"Personal?"

"I was going to say confusing, but personal as well."
How did she explain to Maggie, a true romantic under her
sometimes dowdy exterior, that she'd married without love?
That she'd married because Max had given her no choice, but
that beneath the surface of their relationship currents swirled?
Deep unfathomable currents that were pulling her in, sweeping
her to she didn't know where.

Maggie watched her awhile longer and then nodded. "Well,
whenever you are ready…"

"Thanks."

Maggie sipped her coffee. "What about the professional
side of things? How does marrying Cameron Enterprises'
head of PR affect your work with the *Gazette?*"

"It doesn't. We have an understanding where neither of
us discusses our work." Which fortunately or unfortunately
meant she hadn't felt obliged to tell Max about the article
that would be running in tomorrow's *Gazette.* Another article
questioning Rafe Cameron's motives and intentions.

"That must be hard."

"Not really. I can keep business and pl—personal separate."
She'd been going to say "pleasure." Pure, hedonistic, fiercely
erotic pleasure.

"And yet you claim it's business that's occupying your
thoughts. Clearly your work is far more enthralling than
mine. Is it this wrangle you're getting into with Cameron
Enterprises?"

A wrangle? Probably a good word, or a tangle, and not
with Cameron Enterprises but with Max. Her husband. "It's
really not that interesting." Confusing maybe, mixed with
illicit excitement and a sprinkle of fear. *Don't think about it.
Not now,* she warned herself. She was here to talk to Maggie
and part of the benefit of seeing her friend was the hope that
she could forget her own situation. "From what you said on

the phone, yours is the job that's about to get interesting. Tell me more."

Maggie narrowed her eyes suspiciously but accepted the change of subject. She drew in a deep breath. "Do you know William Tanner?"

"The CFO Rafe brought out from New York as part of his takeover crew."

"Yes. He has an executive assistant in New York but she's handling everything long-distance, and Cameron Enterprises is looking for someone for him who'll be based here."

"And you're applying? That's terrific."

"I'm thinking about it."

"Maggie, you *have* to apply."

"I want to, but it would be such a big step up from the general secretarial work I've been doing."

Gillian watched closely as Maggie cut her bran muffin carefully in half. "You're ready for more of a challenge. We talked about that very thing the last time we had coffee." Maggie was smart and savvy but she hid her light behind a bushel and her looks behind her ill-fitting suits and glasses.

"You're right. I've got the skills."

"So what is it that's holding you back?"

"It's William Tanner. His reputation precedes him." Maggie halved each of the halves again.

"What's wrong with him? Horns, a tail and a red pitchfork?"

Maggie laughed and set her knife down. "Almost. Word is he's tough as nails. His executive assistants don't always last that long—the last two temps filling in for his permanent one when she was away on maternity leave lasted no more than a few weeks each."

"They were temps, you're not. Cameron Enterprises employs only the best. You, being a case in point." Max being another, she thought. "William Tanner will be lucky to get you, because you're smart and capable, and if he has even half a brain he'll realize that pretty darn quickly."

"Thank you."

"For telling you the truth? Anytime." A woman pushing a sleeping baby in a stroller walked past, snagging Gillian's attention.

"Can I tell *you* a truth?"

She didn't like the note of warning she heard in Maggie's voice. "Will you listen to me if I say no?"

"No. Because it's just a little thing but I think you need to hear it."

Gillian sighed. "Go on then."

"I don't know Max real well."

No surprises there, Gillian thought, even when she'd been dating the man for six months she hadn't been able to claim that she knew him well.

"But he has a reputation for being fair and he's good at what he does, and you can talk to him about anything to do with work."

"Go on."

"But from what I hear he's deeply private. He can shut the whole world out. He's a bit like you that way."

Huh? Admittedly, she didn't wear her heart on her sleeve but she wouldn't have said she shut people out.

"You both compartmentalize your lives," Maggie continued. "I guess what I'm trying to say, badly, judging by the look of horror on your face, is don't shut each other out."

Maggie didn't understand. If Gillian didn't wall off a part of her that was safe from Max she could lose everything. It was one thing to share her home and her life with him. She could even share her body; after all, they both had needs.

But her heart?

She had to keep that protected.

* * *

Max lowered himself into his office chair and flicked over the front page of this morning's edition of the *Seaside Gazette*. Gillian's opinion piece took up the top quarter of page two. He read it through once and then again and then for long seconds he just stared at it. She'd done it again. Only this time the betrayal felt personal. Attacking Rafe again, questioning what he was trying to do in this community, was an attack on him, too.

It was his job to make sure public opinion was in their favor, and she was doing her darndest to make sure it wasn't.

While he hadn't expected her to fall into line with his plans just because they were married and sleeping together, he had thought she might at least run things by him before she went to print on them. Professional courtesy?

Just last night when they'd made love she'd clutched at his back. She'd said nothing about preparing to stab him in that same back.

He picked up his phone, dialed her number and went straight through to voice mail. He didn't get it. He'd never met anyone he was so in tune with physically, and he'd thought mentally. And yet she had the capacity to totally surprise him, as though he didn't know her at all.

He glanced at his watch. She'd be at home now for lunch with Ethan. And he had time before his meeting with a local TV station about the upcoming press conference. He made his decision, pocketed his keys and strode out of his office, closing the door behind him.

Fifteen minutes later he opened the door to their home and found her sitting cross-legged on the couch. She wore soft white yoga pants and a tank top. Her laptop was open on her lap. Her eyebrows were drawn together in concentration, she had her hair pulled up in a ponytail and a pencil behind her ear. And she was without a doubt the most captivating woman he'd ever known.

Max cleared his throat and she looked up startled, her lips parting ever so slightly.

Thank goodness Ethan was here or he'd forget all about what he needed to say to her and push her back on that couch. "Where's Ethan?"

"Play date with a friend from preschool. He'll be back at three. Sorry." She shrugged. "I would have let you know if I'd thought you were going to come home to see him."

"I didn't come home to see him."

Her eyes widened.

"And I didn't come home for sex, either."

"Our own play date?" A light danced in her eyes as though she knew now though that that was all he could think about. That in his mind she was already naked and stretched back on that couch, welcoming him home in her own special way.

He had to clear his throat again before he could speak, and furiously tried to concentrate. He was all about self-discipline, self-control. She wasn't going to derail him with sex. "No."

She shut down the screen on her laptop and closed the machine, looking at him expectantly. "So, what did you come home for?" She leaned forward to set her laptop on the coffee table and he realized, to his horror, that she wasn't wearing a bra. He got an earth-stopping view of beautiful breasts and rosy, peaked nipples. "I haven't had lunch yet. We could eat together," she said as she sat back against the couch. Her tank top doing nothing to disguise her nipples.

"No." His refusal was too emphatic. Born of desperation. "I came to talk you about your opinion piece in the *Seaside Gazette*."

"Oh." She stretched. Nonchalant. As though she didn't know precisely what she was doing to him. How hard he was for her. "What about it?" Raising her arms above her head, she pulled the band from her hair. Chestnut locks cascaded over her bare shoulders, grazed her pale neck.

And he was done for. Couldn't think straight. "This is fighting dirty, Gillian."

"I'm just playing the game your way." A sultry smile of victory widened her lips. "Besides, we can talk work afterward."

The final thread of his self-control snapped.

Three strides had him in front of her. Gripping her shoulders, he hauled her upright and kissed her. She tasted of sweet coffee as she melted into him. He broke their kiss only long enough to pull her tank top over her head. In moments they were naked, he'd sheathed himself and he was inside her welcoming heat, driving home, needing her, filling her, overpowered by her, her body tight and hot around him, her legs wrapped about his hips as she met and matched his thrusts.

Ecstasy. Insanity.

Her eyes clouded with a mirror of the passion that gripped him. Her lips were parted, her breathing ragged. The little gasps she made grew quicker, louder, sending him closer to the edge, fighting for control till she came apart in his arms and, overpowered by sensation, he surged into her.

Home.

He held her to him.

In the recesses of his mind he knew that being with her spelled danger. And that the risks were increasing. But when he was with her only she mattered. He didn't have the strength to shut himself off.

As the ripples of satisfaction faded, he knew that soon, before it was too late, he would have to find the strength.

Eleven

Gillian was hoping. Starting to dream. Starting to rely on Max and what they had.

It frightened her—losing the part of herself that had learned not to need him. She needed it back because he didn't want the things she did. The ringing of her phone startled her. She'd been only half paying attention to Ethan as he happily stacked blocks.

"I'm taking you out tonight," the man she'd been thinking about said. "We need to talk. And it has to be somewhere we won't get sidetracked."

Was he blaming her? She had, she admitted, known she'd stopped him from discussing her opinion piece with what happened this afternoon. But she hadn't wanted to argue and she had wanted him. She always wanted him. If he could use that ever-present desire to stop from talking about Dylan then he couldn't exactly take the moral high ground.

"Get a sitter. I'll be home at six to pick you up."

Maybe she ought to be grateful that he wanted to take her out, and partly she was, but did the assumption that she would and could fit in with his plans, regardless of her own, mean that he knew how much she cared for him? "What if I can't, Max? What if Ethan's come down sick?"

She heard his indrawn breath. "What's wrong with him?" he demanded. "Have you taken him to his doctor? Where is he? Why didn't you call me?"

The rush of questions and the note, almost of panic, in his voice had her backtracking. "Nothing's wrong with him. I said *what if.* I wanted you to realize that when a child's involved no day is predictable. Your needs and wants can't always take top priority."

Silence.

"Max? Are you there?"

"Don't worry about going out. I'll be home early."

He'd shut down, shut her out, she heard it in his clipped words, but she wasn't sure whether his anger was directed at her or himself. Something was wrong and she had no idea what, but she suddenly felt that she needed to make amends. "Are you sure?" she asked quietly. "Ethan's fine, he's playing with his blocks, building towers and then knocking them down. And I was speaking to Mrs. McDonald earlier, who was complaining because her bridge evening was cancelled at the last minute, and—" she took a deep breath "—more than that, I'd really like to go out with you." So much for not needing him. "I haven't been out in far too long." And she'd like the chance to talk to him, properly, where they wouldn't, as he'd put it, get sidetracked. By sex.

There was another silent pause. "If you're sure?"

"Yes. I'm sure."

He was home sooner than she'd expected, explaining that he'd pulled out of a twilight golf fundraiser, sending someone else from his department in his stead. He helped Ethan make a tower that was as tall as their son. And then he helped him knock it down.

Leaving the two males in her life playing allowed Gillian more time to get ready than she'd had in years. Time well spent if the look of approval in Max's eyes when she walked down the stairs was anything to go by. She wore a black dress that stopped a little above her knees and fitted close over her curves with a deep vee at the front.

Desire darkened his eyes. Desire and something else, something warmer that called to her. Or was that only her wishful thinking?

At the base of the stairs and in front of Mrs. McDonald he kissed her, slow and gentle. And if it hadn't been for Mrs. McDonald's presence they wouldn't have made it out the door.

They said goodbye, left last-minute instructions and phone numbers and he took her hand as he led her to his car.

But instead of heading to the beachfront where most of the restaurants and cafés were, he headed out of town. "Where are we going?"

"You'll see."

They stopped at a private airfield. A helicopter flight later and they were setting down on a private airfield in L.A. and stepping into a chauffeur-driven limo.

Her curiosity built. "Now will you tell me where we're going?"

For his answer Max poured her a flute of champagne. "You'll see." He wore a black, button-down shirt, with the top button undone. Gillian couldn't help but think of undoing a couple more for him, sliding her hand over his torso. But he'd said they needed to talk and that he didn't want to be sidetracked.

It was her weakness that his mere presence sidetracked her.

She glanced out the window not recognizing the road they were traveling down. "Your parents?"

He shook his head and a smile tugged at his lips. "Be patient. We'll be there shortly."

Fifteen minutes later the limo slowed to a stop and Gillian looked out the window to see a brightly lit storefront. "A bookstore?"

Max nodded, watching her.

Her favorite kind of store. But his confirmation did little to ease her confusion.

The chauffeur opened her door and they stepped out. Doormen flanked the entrance to the store checking invitations. Gillian recognized a CNN reporter and a British diplomat amongst the guests entering ahead of them.

The large plate-glass window displayed a towering stack—high enough to impress even Ethan—of hardback books set against a backdrop of mountains and helicopter silhouettes.

She recognized the book as the release due to go on sale tomorrow morning by her favorite, and a much-respected, foreign correspondent. "This is Tilsby's book launch?"

"I thought you might like it."

She grasped Max's hand, forcing him to stop when he would have kept walking. "I do. Thank you."

He shrugged and tried to start moving again.

Gillian held firm to his hand, interlacing their fingers, and held his gaze with hers. "No. Don't shrug this off. Thank you. I've admired Tilsby for years and was looking forward to his book. I'm…touched that you thought to bring me here." It meant something—that he'd done this for her, something so thoughtful and personal—she just wasn't sure what. He'd said he wanted to talk and they could have done that in Vista del Mar, he hadn't had to put this much effort into an evening for her. But he had.

They approached the short and steadily moving line. Her

hand rested too comfortably in his. "We've never been out in public together before."

He shot her a glance, frowning. "I suppose not."

"So that hasn't been deliberate?"

He stopped and turned to her, his attention on her one hundred percent. "What are you suggesting?"

"Nothing. It had just occurred to me that, like I said, we haven't been anywhere public together. And apart from your family I've met no one important to you. So, I guess I wondered."

"What? That I didn't want to be seen with you?"

She lifted a shoulder.

He shook his head. "When has there even been time?"

"There hasn't," she agreed.

In front of the small crowd he lowered his head and kissed her, lingering and almost sweet. "Never think that. I'm more proud than you can know to be here with you tonight."

The intensity in his voice, as much as his words, reassured her, calmed the hidden nagging fear that she was building a house of cards.

They stayed at the launch party for an hour mingling, sipping champagne and nibbling hors d'oeuvres. Max bought, and got signed for her, Tilsby's book.

After they left the gathering, Max took her to a quietly exclusive hillside restaurant with a spectacular view over the glittering lights of the city.

The maître d' led them to a corner table. Max stood waiting for her to sit. His innate courtesy and chivalry made her feel cherished, physically, if not emotionally. Emotionally, she recognized, they were both still holding back. For her it was protection—though her resolve was crumbling daily. For him it was second nature.

Since they'd left the bookstore Max had become quieter. "Is something bothering you?"

He adjusted the cutlery in front of him, realigning it with the edge of the table. "Should we call Mrs. McDonald to check that Ethan's all right?"

"She'll call if there's a problem."

He nodded, and moved his bread plate a fraction to the left.

"I'll call if you want."

"Up to you," he said with a nonchalance she wasn't buying.

She called Mrs. McDonald, holding eye contact with Max throughout the conversation. She watched him relax, the subtle edge of tension he'd carried since leaving the launch seeped from him as he interpreted from what he could hear that everything was fine back in Vista del Mar.

As she finished the call, Max filled her wineglass with a dark red pinot noir. She waited as he filled his own and raised it in a silent toast to her, waiting for her to clink her glass against his before taking a sip. Thoughts and suspicions that had first taken root during their phone call earlier were springing further to life.

"What was that all about this afternoon? With Ethan?"

He shrugged. "What do you mean?" He picked up a leather-bound menu. "The seafood here is excellent."

"It was almost as though you panicked when you thought he was sick."

Max sent her a look that said "really, don't be ridiculous" but he didn't actually deny anything.

"And just now, wanting to check in with Mrs. McDonald."

"I'm new to this, Gillian. I guess I'm not as relaxed as you are about kids."

She watched him, aware of the way he wasn't quite meeting her gaze. "Children get sick all the time. Teething, stomach flu, ear infection. It's not a bad thing. It's part of their immune systems developing."

"I'm sure they do," he said. He set his menu down and finally looked at her, the intensity in his gaze making his eyes seem even bluer than normal. "What does happen when he's sick? How do you cope? How do you balance it with work?"

"It depends on how sick he is. Sometimes I call on Mrs. McDonald, sometimes I stay with him and work from home, and sometimes I take leave."

"Must be hard."

"I've coped."

"It wasn't a criticism. You've done a remarkable job with him. He's a great kid."

"I know. But thank you."

"There must have been times when it was difficult."

"There've been times when it's been hell juggling everything. But they always pass and they're not that frequent." She realized he'd subtly turned the topic from him and his reaction to the possibility of Ethan being unwell. "Are you sure that's all there was to your reaction this afternoon? It seemed a little more like...panic. Which surprised me."

He sat back in his chair, folded his arms across his chest. His gaze was distant. All in all it was an intimidating, uncommunicative look. Too sexy. Too challenging. But Gillian was good with challenges. She wasn't the type to back off.

"Maybe I overreacted," he said finally. "I guess I'm not used to children." As though that explained everything.

She'd been a journalist long enough to know when someone was hiding something from her. "I think it's more than that. You *never* overreact. That's just not you. And you certainly never let it show."

"Apparently, I did. Maybe you just know me better than most."

"Tell me about your twin."

His eyes narrowed. Surely he'd had to realize she was going to ask about that at some stage.

"This has nothing to do with Dylan." A French-accented waiter materialized at their table to take their orders and Max's relief was palpable. But it was going to take more than that for Gillian to drop the subject he so clearly didn't want to discuss.

She waited till Pierre left. "Tell me about him. Please. What he was like? What happened to him?"

"This isn't the time or the place." Max took another sip of wine.

"I don't think there's ever going to be a right time or place for you. But I need to know that you're not going to panic with Ethan." It was a low blow and it hit its mark.

Anger flashed in his eyes. He set down his wineglass, but his fist remained clenched around the slender crystal stem. "Fine. Dylan died in his sleep of myocarditis caused by a viral infection five days before we turned thirteen. No warning. He went to bed a little off-color. He never woke up." Max recited the words without emotion, his gaze fixed on some point beyond her shoulder. "End of story."

Gillian stared at him. "End of story? That's it?"

"You asked what happened. I told you. And that's more than I've told anyone else outside of the family in the past twenty years."

Gillian was lost for words, unable to truly comprehend the enormity of his loss. She wanted to reach for him but he looked so brittle that she knew her touch wasn't what he wanted, not when he was trying so hard to be so utterly unemotional, so shut down. She settled for questions, trying to find a way in. "How did it affect you? How did you survive?"

"How did it affect me?" One by one he unclenched his fingers from around his wineglass and rested his hand on the table in what she took as a deliberate attempt to at least look relaxed. "What do you think? It destroyed me," he said quietly. "I lost the other half of myself."

"That's why you didn't want children?"

He stared at the liquid in his glass. "Part of me died with him. I lost the capacity to love."

"Lost it or denied it?"

His fingers curled back into a fist. "It's gone, Gillian. I just don't have it in me. So let's drop the subject."

Gillian wasn't going to back off just because he was uncomfortable and uncommunicative. She knew enough to ignore her own discomfort, and she'd known Max long enough to realize that this was something he needed to tell her. For both their sakes. He couldn't shut down on her now. Couldn't deny something that enormous. "At your parents' house there were trophies in the study for tennis for both you and Dylan, and then from later years, trophies for you for swimming."

His jaw looked tight enough to crack rocks on. He unclenched his teeth enough to speak. "I used to play doubles tennis with Dylan. We were good. After he died I stopped playing competitively and took up swimming."

"Why swimming?"

"Because," he said, his gaze fierce, "it was something Dylan did. Not me. For a while I tried to become him to replace him for myself and for my family. And the bonus was that when you're swimming people can't talk to you, can't ask questions, and you can't see the knowledge and pity in their eyes. You can spend hours in silence going up and down the pool."

"Thank you," she said. What else could she say? How did she put a sorrow and sympathy he wouldn't want to know about into words?

"That's it?"

"It's enough. For now."

He sighed his relief. His fist on the table relaxed. Slightly.

Gillian slid her hand over to cover his, relieved when he accepted her touch. She didn't pull back till Pierre brought their appetizers. "Maybe sometime later you could show me some photos of him."

"Maybe."

And that tacit agreement felt like a victory.

Max picked up a fork. "All the photos are at my parents'."

"There's no hurry."

"I had a call from Mom earlier. She wants us to come up next Saturday, anyway. Wants you and Ethan to meet Daniel, and Kristan and her husband, Craig, and their girls."

She watched his eyes. "How do you feel about that?"

"I'm telling you, aren't I?"

Max stood to the side of the stage, just out of sight behind a heavy blue curtain, watching rock star Ward Miller work the audience like the true professional he was. In this case the audience consisted of local journalists and reporters, from papers, gossip magazines, radio and television stations. And some of those journos had internationally syndicated columns.

They sat on the auditorium's seats, notebooks on laps, Dictaphones clutched, cameras clicking, rolling or at the ready, listening to Ward extol the virtues of Hannah's Hope. The publicly stated goal of the charity—named in memory of Rafe's mother—was to improve literacy levels among the disadvantaged in the community, many of whom were immigrant workers, by pairing them with mentors.

And although the underlying motivation behind founding Hannah's Hope had been to improve the public image of Cameron Enterprises, there was no denying it was already making a real and positive difference.

Ward, who was also a friend of Rafe's, was the perfect spokesperson. He gave Hannah's Hope not just profile but credibility because he was already behind one nationally revered charity, the Cara Miller Foundation, a foundation he'd begun after his wife's death from breast cancer.

Today Ward was all about Hannah's Hope. He told of the people already being helped in ways that would assist them, today and potentially for the rest of their lives.

Ward was not only good-looking and photogenic, he also had an undeniable charisma and charm. But what shone from him was his utter sincerity and a belief in this cause.

Max had spoken with him several times now. And he'd never failed to be impressed by his commitment and passion, initially for the Cara Miller Foundation but now also for Hannah's Hope. He seemed to find genuine fulfillment from working with the charities. They'd shared ideas on how to make each of the charities even more successful. Max was interested in most effectively harnessing Ward's star power and Ward was interested in Max's opinions on increasing the Cara Miller Foundation's West Coast presence.

Max surveyed the audience again and found the person he sought. Gillian. She sat listening attentively, her whole focus on Ward. It had almost been a relief to tell her about Dylan. After not speaking of it to anyone other than his mother who occasionally, like Gillian, forced the issue with him.

It had also been a relief that once he'd told her what she wanted to know she'd let the subject rest. He knew that wouldn't be an end to it but that she'd respect the space he needed to keep around it.

He was glad, he realized with a shock, that he'd found her again, had her back in his life. And that he had Ethan, too. More than glad.

She made light of the years she'd spent on her own but they couldn't have been easy. He would do what he could to make it easier for her now that he was on the scene. He wanted to help however he could, however she'd let him.

Just looking at her brought a warmth to Max. He couldn't stop it. Never thought to until it was too late. And as always the warmth was followed by something hotter. He couldn't help but think of how they'd spent last night and of how they'd spend tonight once Ethan was well asleep.

Ward finished the spiel he and Max had worked on and opened the floor up to questions. Gillian's hand shot up and some of the warmth Max had been feeling cooled. She had that look in her eyes, the same one she'd had when she'd probed him about Dylan, as though she already knew something and was going to keep digging till she uncovered it.

They'd agreed they wouldn't talk about work at home. Which effectively meant they didn't talk about work at all. Either of their jobs. Which meant he had no idea what she was thinking about the charity.

Hers wasn't the first question Ward took. But she kept her hand up, reminding him of Heather Spindler from his eighth-grade class who always sat up front, and always had questions for the teacher. And often as not, answers, too.

After Eric from the local radio station it was Gillian's turn. "Mr. Miller. What do you say to the accusations that the Hannah's Hope charity is nothing more than a smoke screen to improve public opinion toward Rafe Cameron and his takeover of Worth Industries?"

The warmth Max had been feeling only moments ago turned to ice.

Twelve

It was thirty minutes before he was alone with her. Thirty minutes during which he had plenty of time to try to figure her out. Even as he'd been ostensibly busy with other things, like getting Ward quickly and safely from the premises, fending off those few even more persistent members of the press who had no respect for personal boundaries.

Maybe he should have seen Gillian's approach coming, her quest for information that wasn't on offer, but he hadn't. At least not from her. The clearly stated purpose of the press conference had been to spotlight Hannah's Hope.

Of course he'd briefed Ward on the potential for that line of questioning because he'd known it could, and probably would, crop up.

But not from her. That was what it kept coming back to. From anyone else it wouldn't have bothered him. He would have accepted those questions as inevitable. From Gillian it felt like sabotage, of a personal nature.

Which meant he cared too much.

Which meant he had to find a way to make it stop.

He'd caught her for a couple of seconds at the end of the conference and asked if she could wait around for him. It was early afternoon and Ethan would be asleep with Mrs. McDonald watching him so she'd blithely, almost happily, agreed.

He approached her now just as she said goodbye to a young man with cameras strapped across his chest like a gunslinger from the Wild West.

She turned to him with a smile.

A smile that in other circumstances would have set his heart racing. In truth, even now, even when he knew it shouldn't, it still affected him.

"Great press conference." She crossed to him. "Better run than most. Ward has the perfect blend of fame, enigma and charm, along with the tragedy in his past. Rafe couldn't have picked anyone better to front Hannah's Hope. Everyone has something to pick up and run with. The gossip mags about his personal life, some of the papers about his return to the music scene and others about the charity. Hannah's Hope should get excellent publicity from it." She sounded almost excited.

"No thanks to you."

Her head jerked back.

"Come on, Gillian. Quit with the feigned surprise. You can't expect me to be pleased with how the press conference went when you were the one asking the thorny questions. You were the one detracting from the good the charity hopes to achieve."

Her smile had gone. "I was doing my job, Max. Just like you were. Just like I've been doing here for the past six months. Someone was going to ask those questions."

"Why didn't you ask me any of them at home?"

Her eyes had narrowed. "Because we've been keeping work

out of our personal relationship. And because we didn't want to have this type of argument in front of Ethan."

Behind them the conference center staff cleared away the lectern and microphones and stacked chairs.

"What are you trying to do to me?" he asked quietly. "Is this some kind of payback?"

He thought he read a glimmer of hurt in her eyes but it was quickly replaced by defiance. She took her time dropping her notepad into her handbag, snapping it shut. She looked back at him, her face carefully neutral. "This isn't about you, Max."

"It is when you publicly detract from what I'm trying to achieve." He wanted this woman, above anyone else, on his side.

"It's about me doing my job properly."

"What are you going to be writing in the *Gazette* tomorrow?"

"You know I'm not going to tell you that. Just as there are things I know you wouldn't tell me."

"You're right but it's not that simple. The difference is that what I'm doing doesn't impact negatively on what you're trying to achieve. Rafe Cameron's trying to do something good for this community but if the people here are suspicious or hostile toward him, it won't work, won't help the very people he's trying to help, people like his parents used to be."

"Is that the official line?"

"It's the truth."

"It may be, but there's more to it than that. Even the truth has two sides."

Someone knocked over a chair behind them. "Let's talk outside." Max gestured to the exit. They walked together out into a bright clear afternoon. By unspoken agreement they headed for the beachfront a block's walk away.

"Despite the fairy-tale dream of Rafe's rags-to-riches story," she said, "some people are worried that in his takeover of Worth Industries he's out for revenge. And I have to say, it seems there might be a case for that. I'm finding very little information on what his intentions with the company are. What it looks like is that Hannah's Hope, for all that it's doing good, is actually just a front. It's my job to at least bring the questions and concerns to light."

Max said nothing. He couldn't. Because she could well be right. Rafe hadn't said as much to him, but Max knew he held a grudge for the way his parents had been treated by the people of Vista del Mar and by Ronald Worth in particular. That directly or indirectly he blamed them for his mother's death.

Max's understanding of the story was that Hannah and Rafe's father, Bob, had worked for Worth Industries till she became pregnant. When her condition became known, they'd been fired because fraternization hadn't been permitted. The young couple had struggled and those struggles only got worse when Hannah developed COPD. And although the cause was never clear, Rafe suspected exposure to contaminants at Worth Industries had led to the disease. Without health insurance, the family couldn't afford treatment. Hannah had died when Rafe was fifteen.

Max and Gillian turned on to the sidewalk that followed the shoreline. In the distance, waves crashed against the bluffs and surged around rocks. "That's the difference between us," Gillian said. "Your job is to convince people to think what you want them to think. It's my job to give them the information I find and then ask them to think for themselves. I did you a favor. I gave Ward the opportunity to dispel the rumors."

When she got all passionate about an argument or a point she wanted to make her eyes shone and energy radiated from her. And that passion kindled memories of other passions. But now wasn't the time to tell her that. Or even think it. She'd think he was trying to distract her. All the same, he took her hand in his, felt hers soften in his clasp and her fingers curl around his. And her touch seemed necessary and right. "Worth Industries was failing." He stuck to the facts, still hoping to persuade her to see things his way. "Someone was going to take it over or it was going to go bust in a big way and then this town would have nothing."

"But if Rafe takes it over and then sells off the parts to the highest bidder, which is the rumor I'm hearing, a rumor which Rafe has done nothing to quell, this town will still have nothing."

"That's not necessarily what's going to happen."

"Isn't it?"

"I'm not in a position to say."

"I'm sure you're not. Doesn't mean you don't know more than you're letting on."

"What I know for certain is that Rafe's a shrewd business-man. If anyone can make a go of turning the company around, it's him."

"If he's motivated to do it."

Which was the key question, and only Rafe knew the answer.

Gillian leaned into Max a little as they walked the path— partly for the shelter he provided from the cool breeze and partly because, despite their disagreement, being here with him like this made her believe everything would be okay. Above them a gull squawked and swooped. With each wash and ebb of waves to the shore, the tension between them eased. "I know our careers throw up conflicts but we can navigate them." They had to.

"What if you could stop?" he asked.

"Stop what? Do you mean stop highlighting the fact that there are two sides to any story?" she asked gently. He wouldn't really expect that of her.

"No. Stop working for the *Gazette*. Stay home and look after Ethan."

She halted, pulling her hand from his clasp so she could turn to face him. The wind lifted and blew her hair as she stared at him.

"You said yourself that at times, like when he's sick, it's hard."

"As it is for all parents."

"I'd support you. You know money's not an issue. It never will be. And it might be best for Ethan."

Gillian tried to absorb the enormity of what he was suggesting. "You're serious?"

"Completely. It's the perfect solution."

"I ask a few questions you don't like and you want me to give up my job."

"It's not that. I've been thinking of it since the book launch. Thinking it might be the best way forward for us."

"Us? You mean you?"

He shook his head. "No. I meant us."

The scary thing was that he looked and sounded as though he really meant it. The even scarier thing was that for a fleeting moment the idea had held a glimmer of appeal. It wasn't something she could allow. It wasn't something she wanted for myriad reasons. "Max, no matter how perfect your solution may seem to you, I can't ever let myself be totally dependent on you." She spoke slowly, hoping that gave her words the weight she wanted. "I like my job with the *Gazette*. It's the best paper I've ever worked for. What I do there gives me purpose and it keeps me sane. And more than that I need the independence it gives me."

"It's a thought. At least give it some consideration. I'm not suggesting you make an immediate decision."

Had he even heard what she'd said? Gillian turned back. "I'm not going to give up working there. Ever." She hated that her voice shook. "Why don't you give up working for Rafe? There'd be no conflicts of interest then." She started walking.

"You're angry?" He fell into step beside her and reached for her hand.

"Yes."

He interlaced their fingers. "Are you going to yell?"

Their shoulders brushed. "Maybe. If you bring it up again."

It was another minute before he spoke again. "Would we get to have angry sex?"

She bit her lip. This was not funny. She would not laugh. She caught a faint trace of his cologne. He tugged her a little closer. "Maybe angry sex *after* I've yelled at you."

"You could yell during."

"This isn't a joke, Max."

"I wasn't joking."

Max stepped into Rafe's office, passing Chase Larsen on his way out. William Tanner, the CFO, was already seated across from Rafe's desk and, judging by the seriousness of the expressions on the two men's faces, something was up.

"Shut the door behind you," Rafe said. Another bad sign. Rafe always kept his door open.

Max pushed the door closed and took a seat. "What's wrong?"

Rafe nodded at Will, who turned to Max. "I can't be certain just yet but we thought I should give you a heads up."

Max waited.

"I've only just come back from the New York office so I've only had a preliminary look through the Worth Industries accounts but it appears that there are some…discrepancies."

"What do you mean?"

"Funds that aren't correctly accounted for," Will said.

"Accounts that look unnecessarily…padded, figures that don't quite add up."

This was bad. "You're saying…"

"There are two obvious possibilities. The first is that it could be due to clerical and system errors. They implemented some company-wide, accounting policy changes six months ago. So it could be they haven't been handled consistently. In which case the money will still be in the company, just not attributed to the right places."

"And the second possibility?" Max asked.

"Someone's helping themselves to a little extra on the company." Will's expression hardened.

"An inside job?" Max considered the implications.

Will nodded.

"Who and how much?"

"It's too early to answer either of those questions. There are a limited number of people with the necessary access to the accounts to achieve something like this but I don't want to go pointing the finger till we know for certain that it's fraud, and if it is, till I know for certain who could have done it."

Max let the seriousness of the potential ramifications sink in.

Rafe leaned forward. "We've brought you in at this stage because—"

"Because if it is fraud, and that knowledge gets out into the public, as it inevitably will, the PR implications for the company are huge." The press, including Gillian, would have a field day with it.

The two other men nodded, faces solemn.

"Looks like I'd better start working on a crisis management plan. Give me your worst-case scenario."

Max sat across the table from his son that evening, watching him eat. But tonight his thoughts weren't totally on Ethan or even Gillian. They were back with Cameron Enterprises. He had never met a crisis he couldn't work through, and usually he loved the challenge of it. But this was different. Someone stealing from the company—the thought appalled him.

Gillian stood mixing something at the sink, swaying gently to the pop tune on the radio. She'd feel the same. She turned. Caught him watching. "Is everything okay?"

"Great."

Only it wasn't. And part of the "not" okay was the fact that he couldn't talk about this with Gillian. Not tonight, or tomorrow. Not until if and when it became necessary to make the knowledge public.

And that should have been okay. If this had happened last month he wouldn't have had Gillian to talk through ideas with. So why did it matter now that he not only couldn't talk it through with her, he had to hide it from her, something that was going to consume a lot of his mental energies until it was sorted?

After Ethan was in bed Max went to his room and opened up the laptop on the desk. He wasn't sleeping in here anymore—Gillian's bed had so much more to offer, a warm willing body, her laughter and her loving—but he used this room if he had to work from home.

Home?

He knew the power of words. And he knew that this house with its precious inhabitants had already become more of a home than he'd allowed himself in his adult life.

The thought ought to worry him. He ought to stop it.

He looked up at the sound of a tap on the door. Gillian stood with her head tilted to one side. It was her figuring things out look. "Is something wrong?"

"No." Other than his endless longing for her.

Her olive-green, scoop-neck T-shirt hugged her curves, revealing just the start of the swell of her breasts.

"You seemed a little distracted this evening."

"There's a lot of stuff happening with work." He shut down the screen on the laptop. Knew she saw him do it, knew she knew the reason, that there were things there he didn't want her to see.

"Oh." There it was. The barrier between them. "I had thought I might come in and…" Her gaze flicked to the bed. "But you're busy. I'll—"

"Don't." He wanted, more than anything, for her to stay. He pushed away from the desk and crossed to her. "I hate that there are things I can't share with you."

"It's okay. I understand."

"I know you do. Doesn't mean I like it."

"Don't bring up the job thing again, my resigning from the *Gazette*."

He shook his head. "I wasn't going to." She'd convinced him of its importance to her. He slid his hands beneath the hem of her T-shirt, rested his palms against the warmth of her waist. He wasn't certain, but he thought her waist, the soft feminine curve of it, might just be his favorite part of her body. The concave curve that had once swollen with his child. He loved that he was free to touch her, felt a fierce pride in how willingly she came to him, how quickly she responded to him.

"The *Gazette* is the furthest thing from my mind." He tugged her closer, kissed the pale skin of her neck, worked his way past her earlobe, along her jaw, till he found her lips. She tasted ever so faintly of the mint chocolate chip ice cream they'd shared for dessert. Only so much better. Far more tempting. Far headier and more decadent.

He walked backward, bringing her with him till he reached the bed.

* * *

Gillian looked up into Max's eyes, saw a heart-stopping, heart-melting warmth in their blue, blue depths. She looped her arms around his neck, wanting, needing to get closer to him, to show him that the world didn't matter, that it wasn't something she'd let come between them.

She pressed her body to the length of his, thighs to thighs, hips to hips, feeling his hardness, responding deep within her to his nearness, to the promise of pleasure. His beautiful lips curved into a smile of aching tenderness. And she slid up against him on tiptoe to kiss him. She let her longing for him lace the kiss.

Lips joined, he peeled her T-shirt from her, breaking the kiss only long enough to complete its removal and drop it to the floor. Her bra followed. Still kissing her, he stroked and smoothed his hands all over her as though he wanted to touch and learn each and every inch, skimming up her sides, over her shoulders, paying reverent attention to her breasts, her nipples. His hands lowered, kneaded her behind, pulling her closer as he did so, then he slid his hands between them to unfasten her pants. Together, they pushed them down her hips, and she stepped out of them and then turned her attention to the privilege and delight of getting him equally naked. Of revealing his torso, stripping his pants from his lean hips, down over powerful thighs. Of delighting in his readiness for her.

They fell onto the bed together and lay facing each other. Gillian nudged him with her bottom leg and he lifted his hips enough that she could slip that leg beneath him, fit it below his waist, her other leg completing the circle in which she held him. She angled her hips, needing him to fill her, to become one with her. Slowly, he slipped the hard length of him inside her, filling her exquisitely then withdrawing torturously to then fill her again. And all the while he looked into her eyes, his own darkened and glazed with arousal, his beautiful lips parted.

They made love slowly, languidly, tenderly. It was almost dreamlike—except for the pleasure. The pleasure was intense and real, enthralling her, claiming her, overwhelming her. She touched Max's face, felt the gentle rasp of his strong jaw against her palm. She could stay like this forever. With the man she loved. That one forbidden thought—love—cut through the sensual magic and then sank again, swamped by bliss.

A bliss that was irresistible. Their rhythm quickened, gathered force, and still the pleasure built till it was almost too much to be borne, escaping in low moans and gasps. Their beautiful rhythm made music that was theirs alone, music that climaxed as she clenched and shattered around him. He followed her completion, burying himself deep within her.

Thirteen

Something had changed with yesterday's lovemaking. Something Gillian couldn't quite bring herself to examine.

Not yet.

She sat beside Max in the luxury of his car, Ethan in the back as they headed to Beverly Hills and Max's family. "You okay?" he asked, attuned to her quietness, if not to the reason for it. "We don't have to do this."

Gillian pulled her gaze from the window. "We probably do. Your entire family is going to be there, aren't they?"

"Yeah. Doesn't mean we can't pull out if you want to."

She wasn't as apprehensive about this, their second meeting, as she had been about their first. Though she knew she'd still be under scrutiny. There would be more questions.

But she'd liked his family that first time. Surely that wouldn't have changed. And the key difference was her relationship with Max. The first time they'd been there had been the same day they'd gotten married.

She hadn't known where she stood with him, how their relationship could possibly work.

In the intervening weeks he'd moved into not only her home and her life but into her mind. She couldn't think about her heart, couldn't afford to consider the possibility that he was making inroads there, too.

The one facet of the whole arrangement that didn't give her trouble was the relationship between Ethan and Max. Ethan adored him and the feeling seemed mutual.

"It's not your family that's bothering me."

"What is?"

What she had no gauge of was how he felt about her.

He cherished her, doing little things unasked for her, helping with Ethan, and he thought of her, he said as much each night as he stripped her clothes from her, but it was more than sex, too. It was something deeper. Surely taking her to Tilsby's book launch had proved that he thought about the things she liked. Surely the tenderness with which they made love... Or was she just desperate that her feelings for him not be totally one-sided?

Like last time. When she'd assumed their relationship was not only strong but going somewhere.

"Us."

"Us?" She heard his wariness.

"Where's our relationship going?" It was the dead last thing she should blurt out like that, but that was one of her problems, her tendency to speak what was on her mind.

Max slowed as the area around them became more built up. She didn't know if she was imagining it or not, but his grip on the wheel looked tighter than before.

"Forget I asked. I know what we have and don't have. I knew how it would be when I agreed to marry you."

"But you want more?" he asked.

"No."

They both knew she was lying.

"Mommy," Ethan called, a plaintive note to his voice.

She turned in her seat. "We're nearly there, honey, then you'll be able to get out and run around, and you'll see Uncle Jake." Uncle Jake had made by far the biggest impression on Ethan. "He's looking a little pale," she said to Max. "Maybe he's carsick."

"Shall I stop?"

"How long till we get there?"

"Less than ten."

"I think he'll be okay." Gillian stayed turned in her seat watching Ethan, who seemed, now that he had her full attention, to be fine.

"Huh," Max said when eventually they slowed and drove through the gates of his parents' home.

Gillian looked up the driveway and then back at Max. "Seems like a lot of cars."

"The whole clan is definitely here."

Laura came out to meet them as they got out of the car. "You made it. Good trip? And how's my favorite grandson?" She held out her arms to take Ethan from Max.

"I don't know that he's feeling so good," Gillian said.

"Nonsense," Laura said, reaching for Ethan. "He looks fine." Various other family members had come out of the house and stood on the front doorstep, watching expectantly. At which point Ethan threw up.

Gillian stood on the back lawn with Max's sister, Kristan, watching Ethan, who was now fully recovered from his bout of travel sickness and playing happily with Kristan's six-year-old daughters, Lilly and Nicole. They were taking turns pushing him around the lawn in a bright yellow car.

She and Kristan had hit it off straight away. Kristan winning a place in Gillian's heart with her calm, efficient help in getting Ethan cleaned up, as well as the stories she'd shared of similar and worse incidents with her girls. Gillian had sat by Kristan during lunch, giving her someone to talk to who wasn't completely obsessed by baseball.

Ethan's squeals of laughter drew her attention. And beyond Ethan she saw Max and Laura standing talking, both of them occasionally glancing her way till Max, his jaw tight, left his mother's side to stand beside Gillian. She should never have asked what she did about their relationship.

"Is everything all right?" she asked.

"Fine." He lifted a shoulder. "Mom's given me the CD with the photos on them, that's all."

"The photos of Dylan?" Perhaps that was the explanation for his tension. "Can I see them?"

"Here? Now?"

"Yes." If not now he'd find some other excuse to delay showing them to her. "Ethan's fine and Kristan and the girls are watching him."

The muscle in his jaw up by his ear worked. "Sure," he said with a nonchalance that she didn't for a minute believe. He led her to a media room at the back of the house and set the CD up to play and started to give her instructions for the remote and the screen.

"You're going to look at them with me, aren't you?"

He hesitated.

"Please. I'll need you to explain them. To tell me about him."

"They're annotated."

She looked at him till finally he shrugged and sat on the couch beside her.

Surprising her, he slipped his arm around her shoulder.

After the things they'd shared and done together it made no sense that that simple gesture, his arm over her shoulders, the two of them close on the couch, should make her heart swell. But it did. "Are you ready?" she asked.

"Whenever," he said easily, though without enthusiasm.

The slideshow of pictures was in chronological order, starting with a massively pregnant Laura, progressing through photos of two tiny babies in matching blue outfits but with different colored knitted hats. "Identical?" Gillian asked.

He shook his head. "Fraternal, but people outside the family still had trouble telling us apart."

Through the years the boys grew and changed, becoming more distinct. The photos showed birthdays and Christmases as well as school productions. There were shots of them climbing trees like monkeys, scaling walls and diving from a cliff into a lake. Photos that had Gillian's heart in her mouth just looking at them. "You must have turned your parents gray."

Max smiled. "We had no fear. We thought we were invincible." And there were sporting endeavors often culminating in one or both of them holding a trophy.

"Competitive?"

He smiled. "Intensely."

Then, finally, abruptly, just after one of Max and Dylan with their arms slung about each other, there was a photo of a funeral, and then one of a granite headstone surrounded by flowers. Her heart ached with grief for a boy she'd never known.

They sat in silence and as the screen went blank the room darkened. "I didn't know what to do with myself after he died," Max said. "I'd always been half of a pair. I didn't know who I was anymore." He stood abruptly, crossed to the drapes.

"How did you cope?" she asked before he pulled them back because that would flood the room with light and she knew it would be easier for him to talk in the darkness.

"I went through all the stages of grief—anger, denial, guilt, over and over. In the end I figured out I was never going to get over it but that I couldn't let it beat me. I would go on… with the emptiness inside."

She didn't know what to say. She couldn't comprehend the depth of his loss. He opened the drapes and headed for the door. Gillian caught up to him there. He looked at her, almost challenging her with his gaze to say something, undoubtedly the wrong thing. All she could think to do was to reach for his hand and count it a small victory that he kept it in his as they rejoined his family.

Kristan passed Gillian a glass of wine. "Here, you look like you could use this." She dropped down beside Gillian on the low couch, her own glass carefully balanced. On the floor in front of them, Lilly and Nicole were putting a fairy dress on Ethan.

Max had agreed to Laura's request that they stay for dinner. Gillian couldn't help but feel that he'd agreed in order to avoid spending time alone with her.

Had getting him to show her the photos of Dylan been a mistake? Had she pushed him too far? She felt like she was feeling her way blindfolded. The right steps could lead her to safety and the wrong steps could take her over a precipice.

She seemed to be making blunder after blunder today where Max was concerned, questions about where their relationship was going, questions about Dylan, but she'd thought she was doing an okay job of concealing her disquiet. "I look that bad, huh?"

"I didn't mean it like that." Kristan took a sip of her wine.

Gillian raised her glass in thanks. "I know you didn't. But you're right, anyway. It's been a long day." Kristan and her girls had been one of the bright spots. Not only had the girls reveled in having a young cousin to mother but Ethan had basked in their attention.

"There were quite a few questions coming your way over lunch."

A subtle barrage but she'd coped. "I usually prefer to be the one asking them than the one answering them. Did I do okay?"

Kristan laughed. "You were fine. You fit right in. And you've won Mom's everlasting gratitude by getting Max to look at the photos."

"You heard?"

"That news went round the family like wildfire. Max hardly ever talks about Dylan or looks at the photos. We're so glad he can with you. You and Ethan are so good for him. I thought he might never let himself love again."

Gillian said nothing. *Love* wasn't a word Max would consider. But perhaps, she hoped, he felt something for their son. She tried to take heart from Kristan's ill-informed interpretation of the situation. Perhaps one day they could have…something.

Ethan's gurgling laughter as he danced and spun in the fairy dress sent Lilly and Nicole into peals of giggles. "He's a lovely little boy," Kristan said, breaking into her thoughts.

"He's certainly enjoying playing with your two."

"They do enjoy company. All children do."

Gillian knew where this subject inevitably led and took another sip of her wine.

"Any plans for number two?"

She should issue a quick denial. But watching Ethan with the twins she couldn't help but wondering, and wishing just a little.

Kristan smiled. "I can see it in your eyes."

"I always wanted more than one child. Maybe two or three

or who knows…" The warmth and closeness of Max's family could make her want and wish for all sorts of things.

"And you don't want the age gap to be too big." Kristan's blue eyes, so like Max's, held a teasing glint.

"I suppose not." But Max, for whom one child had been a shock and an adjustment, was far from ready to consider such a prospect. From the time they'd resumed a physical relationship, he'd taken careful responsibility for birth control. And their relationship was far too tenuous and new to introduce that sort of pressure. Or even the discussion of the possibilities. She could just imagine how he would shut down and shut her out.

Kristan was watching her so closely that Gillian looked away for fear that she would reveal her doubts and uncertainties. Her gaze caught on a pair of long masculine legs, traveled up over hips and a torso she knew intimately, and stopped when they met the other blue eyes she'd just been thinking of.

There was no teasing glint in Max's eyes.

If anything, she'd call the look she saw there, accompanied by the twist to his lips, surprise or maybe…horror.

Max turned on his heel.

Ten minutes later he'd yet to come back. Gillian finished her wine and her glance strayed to the doorway he'd left through.

"He's probably playing pool with Carter," Kristan said gently. "The pool room is down the end of that hallway on the right. I'll watch Ethan."

Had Kristan seen the look on her brother's face? She hadn't mentioned it and nothing obvious had changed in her demeanor, but…

Gillian turned her wrist to look at the time that now crawled by. "I might just go see…" she could think of no plausible excuse "…him."

The pool room was a masculine hideout with its wood-paneled walls lined with sporting paraphernalia and a well-stocked bar in the far corner. Max bent low to the pool table, the cue resting on the fingers of his outstretched hand. His other arm was drawn back. With a smooth precise movement the cue slid forward, sent the white ball into the black with a click. The black rolled to the corner and dropped into the pocket.

"Merciless," Carter said from where he stood a little back from the pool table, the end of his cue resting on the ground, his hands stacked one on top of the other where they clutched the tip. "What's up with you today, anyway?" He looked around the room and noticed Gillian. "Oh," he said on a sigh of understanding. He held his cue out to her. "Your turn? I'm done being slaughtered here."

Max had straightened to watch her. Waiting for her to decline Carter's offer. But this, she realized, might be the perfect opportunity to talk to him. She shrugged and reached for Carter's cue. "Good luck," he said with a wink before strolling from the room.

Max racked up the balls in the triangle. "You want to break?"

"Why not? I get the feeling it might be my best chance against you."

He straightened. "Carter exaggerated."

"Your ability or your mood?"

"Both." He stepped back from the table, gestured with an open palm for her to take her shot.

"I haven't played in a long time."

"I didn't know you'd played at all."

Just another example of all that was unknown and uncertain between them. "Only enough to know the basics."

She leaned low and drew her arm back. Sensation tingled and she glanced back to see Max watching her. Trying to block out the disconcerting intensity of his scrutiny, she retrained her gaze along her cue. She played her shot, sending the white into the side of the triangle of balls, scattering them haphazardly. And sinking none of them.

Max walked the length of the table, stopping at the far end. He made his shot, sinking first one and then a second ball.

"Are we going to talk?" she asked.

"Nothing to talk about." He moved along the table, his concentration absolute. He leaned down to line up his next shot, a frown creasing his brow.

"I don't think Carter exaggerated."

She wasn't even certain he'd heard her. She needed to get through to him, needed to find a chink in his armor. Gillian leaned opposite him, resting her forearms on the edge of the table so that when he sighted along his cue he got a view of her gently gaping blouse, a glimpse of the cream lace beneath it.

His frown deepened. "At least Carter doesn't play dirty." But he looked a little longer before taking, and missing, his shot.

It was her turn and Gillian leaned over the table.

"Nice," Max murmured from where he stood behind her.

She felt him move nearer, felt his hands close around her hips. She played her shot—badly—sinking nothing, then set her cue down, straightened and turned to him, recognizing the heat in his eyes.

"I can lock the door."

If she said yes she would bridge the distance between them. They would connect—physically, but it would be a way of avoiding rather than dealing with what was bothering him. "We can't keep using sex to gloss over things between us."

His hands skimmed her hips and waist, slid up till he linked his fingers behind her neck. "We can."

Already she felt herself responding to his touch. "You heard what I said to Kristan?"

He released her and stepped back.

"About wanting more children."

Max picked up his cue and studied the table. He bent and drew back his arm.

"I didn't mean for you to hear that."

He sank the red ball cleanly.

"I do want more children. But it's hypothetical."

He sank another ball and lined up his next shot.

Gillian stepped in to cover the white ball with her hand, forcing him to pay attention. "It's not like I'm ready or even thinking of more children now or ever. It's just a wish. Like wanting world peace. I know things are far too uncertain between us to bring another child into the mix. I know you're not ready." She slid the ball back and forth across the green baize. "I know that you might never be. And I'm okay with that." Finally, she let go of the ball and looked at him.

"Thank you." The words were clipped. He played his shot.

Instead of reassuring him, all she'd achieved was to drive a wedge further between them.

She hadn't expected him to say anything encouraging, give some kind of hint that one day, perhaps, they could be a proper family, because that wasn't what he wanted. But damn it, her foolish heart had hoped anyway. The foolish heart that was just laying itself open to be trodden on.

She turned from the table and placed her cue back in the rack.

The dawning awareness that she'd been trying to hold at bay—like resisting an incoming tide—crashed through her defenses.

She loved him.

She loved him with every breath she took. Loved everything about him. His strengths and his wounds, his honor and humor and passion. And he wanted to withhold all that from her.

Wanted to shut himself off. To give her only meager parcels of who and what he was, who and what he could be, if only he let himself.

Her throat tightened.

Behind her, she heard the door open and close.

Fourteen

Their trip back to Vista del Mar was strained and silent. As soon as they'd put Ethan to bed, Max went out.

Gillian listened for his return and ached for a way to close the distance she'd brought between them. It was late before she heard his tread on the stairs. He hesitated outside her door. Since they'd first resumed their physical relationship he'd slept every night in here with her. She held her breath—let it out when finally, finally, her door swung open.

And when she turned to him in the darkness and they made love, she tried to give him with her body and her touch what he wouldn't let her give him in words.

He'd made it clear from the outset that his love wasn't on offer. But surely hers was her domain, her right to feel and to give.

It wasn't as though she'd intended to fall in love with him. It had happened on its own, like a seed that had fallen into the earth where no one expected it to grow that germinated and flourished till it was a living, thriving thing that wouldn't be denied. One moment she'd thought there was no room in her heart for anyone other than Ethan and the next, this man was there. Max.

He might not want to hear the words, but she could think them. She couldn't not. Couldn't deny the fundamental, lonely truth of them.

He didn't have to love her back. It would be unfair to expect that, even if she couldn't stop a rebellious corner of her heart hungering for it regardless.

"Where's Daddy?" Ethan asked as she tucked him into bed three days later.

"He's at work, honey." It might have been the truth or it might not. Work was certainly the reason he'd given Gillian for his long absences. But given that the extended hours dated from that day at his parents' she had to assume there was more to it than just work.

He left early in the morning. Usually came back for dinner with Ethan, and then went out again. Tonight he hadn't even made it back for dinner or bath time. Ethan had asked twice already for him.

It was hard to see it as anything other than a rejection of her. Not Ethan, she knew it wasn't that, though she only hoped their son wasn't picking up on Max's tension around her.

She turned at the sound of footsteps to see Max filling Ethan's doorway.

"Hi." His greeting encompassed both her and Ethan. He walked slowly in and sat on the bed beside her.

"Read me a story, please, Daddy."

Gillian watched his face, tried to read his body language. "I've just finished one, so you don't have to if you don't have time."

His gaze narrowed on her. "Of course I have time." He

turned to Ethan. "Which do you choose, *Goodnight Moon* or *The Little Yellow Digger?*"

"The Digger, The Digger."

"Okay, then." He started reading, finding the gentle rhythm of the story. By the time he got to the end of the book Ethan's eyes were drifting closed.

Gillian and Max stood. She leaned down to hug and kiss their son. "I love you, Ethan."

He wrapped his arms around her neck. "I love you, Mommy."

Max bent down to kiss him. "I love you, Daddy," Ethan said as he hugged Max.

She saw Max's arms tighten around Ethan but he said nothing. Ethan had no expectation of a response so didn't notice its absence as he pulled his blue blanket up under his cheek.

Gillian and Max walked down the stairs.

On the bottom stair she stopped. "And, Max."

He turned back to her, his face blank.

"I love you, too." She couldn't go on pretending she didn't. She needed to say the words out loud. Needed him to hear them from her. Unlike Ethan, she did have an expectation of a response, or a reaction, something, anything. More than the working of a muscle in his jaw. She tried to make it easy for him, tried to find a way to make this work, to get past the dread in his expression. "I know you might never love me back," she said quietly. "But that's okay. Really it is. Just don't leave us."

"I'm not leaving. I told you that when I moved in here."

"I meant emotionally. Please. Ethan needs you. And I need you."

Max studied her, a mix of horror and pain in his expression. He backed away from her till his hand rested on the door handle.

"Stay."

"I have to go out."

Looked a lot like leaving—running—to her.

Gillian watched him go. Prayed for him to stop and turn around. As he got into his car and drove away, the gaping hole in her chest yawned wider. She'd thought she could do this, love enough for both of them. She'd thought she could give love and not need it back. Her jaw tightened and her throat locked up.

The blood still rushed in his ears and his heart still pounded as Max sat on the high stool at the far end of the bar at the Beach and Tennis Club.

"Whiskey," he said a minute later when he looked up from the polished mahogany to see the bartender waiting in front of him.

The murmur of conversation rose and fell around him. Upbeat music played through the sound system, a prelude to a night of socializing and dancing for the club's patrons.

Upbeat was the last thing he felt.

His whiskey arrived and he stared into the golden-brown liquid. For a time, in his late teens, he'd tried drinking as a way to deal with his problems. It hadn't worked then. And he knew it wouldn't work now.

But it might make the problems go away for a while.

He took a sip, savored the slow warmth. How had it come to this? He'd had a plan. A good plan. Marry Gillian, be a father to Ethan, be a presence in their lives.

But not their hearts.

He didn't want them to need him or love him. And worse, he didn't want to need or love them back. He *couldn't* love them back.

He carried his glass across to the wide windows, to stand in a dimly lit corner. Night had fallen and the other patrons had turned away from the dark vista of the ocean. Max welcomed that forever endlessness. Yet still it felt as though walls were closing in on him and a band was tightening around his chest.

"Didn't expect to see you here."

He turned at the sound of Chase Larson's voice.

"I heard you'd gotten married."

Max glanced at his left hand and the gold ring on his finger. "Yeah."

"Congratulations. Everything going all right?"

Which Max translated as "What the hell are you doing drinking alone in a bar when you have a beautiful wife and son at home waiting for you?" And she would be waiting. And she would ask no questions, make no accusations. She offered only acceptance and warmth and understanding. And love.

And he didn't want that.

He wanted barriers. He wanted protection. He wanted things to be simple.

But none of that was anything he was prepared to discuss with Chase. He glanced beyond Chase, saw his pregnant wife, Emma, sitting and laughing at a table with several other people. She had that glow that being deeply in love gave some women.

Unlike the look that supposedly being in love with him gave Gillian. A look of someone waiting for bad news.

"Emma's doing okay?" Just two months ago Emma had been involved in a car crash.

"She and the growing baby bump are doing great." Warmth suffused Chase's voice and face. Turned out men could get that same madly-in-love look. Max shook his head. Who knew.

Chase raised the glass of orange juice he held. "I'd better get this over to her."

"Sure. Good talking to you." Max hid his relief. He needed thinking time.

"You, too." Chase turned, stopped and turned back. "I might be out of line here but…well, life can be pretty unpredictable. You never know what's around the corner. Finding and then almost losing Emma has taught me to appreciate every day, every minute, every second I have with her."

"I'm glad for you." Really, he was.

Chase's smile was pitying. "You're a smart man. You'll figure it out." He strolled toward Emma's table.

Max looked back down at his whiskey. He, more than anyone, knew how unpredictable life could be. How someone could be ripped from you before you'd even stopped to think about how much they meant to you.

Gillian shouldn't have said what she did. She shouldn't have said she loved him. For all the world he didn't want to hurt her. He'd warned her.

He caught his reflection in the glass, saw for an instant Dylan's eyes. Dylan who'd been afraid of nothing, who teased and pushed. And his brother laughingly whispered "coward" in his ear.

Coward?

The sounds of the bar ebbed and flowed around Max, leaving him in a pocket of utter stillness and clarity. Comprehension rushed in, overpowering the denial.

It wasn't Gillian he was afraid of hurting.

It was, he understood with blinding clarity, about protecting the shell of a life he'd been living. It was about fear.

His fear of loving.

That was why he'd fought the rising tide of emotions he felt for her. Because he didn't want to feel anything at all. Because the greater the love, the greater the pain of loss.

But if he carried on behaving like an idiot—doing the very thing he'd assured her he'd never do, proving all her initial doubts about him right—he *would* lose her. And that loss would be insurmountable.

Because he loved her, whether he'd wanted to or not.

This feeling he'd fought so hard to deny pulsed through him with every beat of his heart, permeated him with every breath he took.

Love.

She'd offered it tonight and he'd walked away from it. From her. From a woman who was so much more than he deserved.

He turned from the window and raced for the door.

He had to get back to her.

And he had to find a way to convince her he was staying. For good.

Mrs. McDonald, knitting in hand, had come over as soon as Gillian called her. She'd been going quietly insane stuck inside the house waiting—hoping—for Max's return.

She drove slowly to the beach and parked in the same lot she and Max had used when he'd brought her here for a picnic.

The view over the darkened sea was supposed to help give her perspective.

It did. But small and insignificant wasn't the perspective she'd wanted.

How did she find a way forward from here? For herself and for Ethan and for Max. She should never have questioned where their relationship was going, she should never have given voice, even in private, to her wish for more children. But most of all she shouldn't have told him she loved him. She had broken all the rules.

A dark gleaming sedan pulled alongside her car. She muttered her irritation with the lone driver. The whole deserted lot and he had to park right beside her. The driver got out.

Max?

He tugged on the handle of her locked passenger door. She

considered ignoring him but what would that achieve except prolong the inevitable? He had something he wanted to say to her. She may as well let him get it over with.

Taking a deep breath, she hardened herself against him and pressed the button for the central locking. Max opened the door and a chill wind swept in. He eased in beside her and shut the door. Shutting out the wind, shutting her in the confined space of her car with him and bringing with him the faint scent of Eternity.

"What are you doing here?" Wasn't that the very same question she'd asked him the first time she saw him just a few short weeks ago? Weeks that would turn her life upside down and inside out.

"We need to talk."

And that could well have been his same answer. An answer that back then had sent her world careening down the unforeseen path. What new path would tonight's "talk" send them down? She could hardly bear to think. "You don't need to say anything."

"Yes, I do. And you need to listen to it. I've made some changes."

Her heart plummeted. A path over a precipice? She stared straight ahead. Even though the engine wasn't running and she was going nowhere, she gripped the wheel. It gave her something to hold on to. The illusion of control. *Please just let him get this over with quickly.* She waited, frowning at the ocean.

"I bought a new car. Actually, I bought two. I have a friend who's a dealer."

That statement was so vastly different from what she'd been expecting, so seemingly inappropriate, that she turned to him for verification.

What was she supposed to say? *How nice for you.* The car's badge glinted in the glow from the streetlight.

He studied her face. "They've both got four doors," he said as though that was supposed to mean something.

This was getting stranger and stranger. Surely he hadn't tracked her to here to tell her about his nighttime vehicle purchases.

Max looked up at the roof for a second. "I'm not doing this right."

"If I'm supposed to understand what you're talking about then no, you're not doing it right."

"The day I first moved in with you I asked what it would take to make you believe that I was going to stay. One of things you said was trading in the coupe for something more suitable for a child. I did."

She remembered that conversation, remembered how back then she hadn't thought he had what it would take to be a part of their lives.

"And it's a hybrid. Better for the environment. I'm thinking of the future. Of all our children and of our grandkids."

Of all our children and of our grandkids. Now, darn it, hope was flickering. "You're not leaving?"

"How many times do I have to tell you that?" he asked gently. "No, I'm not leaving. Not today. Not tomorrow. Not ever."

"I thought I'd panicked you with…what I'd said."

"That you love me?"

She nodded.

His smile was soft. "You did. But in a good way—eventually. In a way that forced me to think things through and come to some realizations and to make some decisions about us and about our future."

She could feel her heart beating but she held tight to the fact that he was using words like *us* and *future* and the hope burned a little brighter.

"I've hated not being able to share things, like what's

happening at work, with you. And I don't want our jobs to come between us."

"I could look for something new," she said tentatively. If he was saying what she thought he was, if he was holding out hope for her, she'd do whatever it took to grasp hold of it. What they could have was worth any price.

He touched her face, reverence in the brush of his fingertips. "You love your job and there's not much else like that around here. On the other hand, as part of my work with Hannah's Hope I've been talking with Ward about the Cara Miller Foundation a lot lately. It's got me thinking that that side of things is something I'd like to be involved in." His thumb stroked her jaw. "I could bring a lot to it. They're looking at opening an office on the West Coast. It may take a little time but once I find someone to take over for me with Rafe I'm moving over to the foundation. You can stay with the *Gazette* and keep doing what you do so infuriatingly well."

She leaned into his palm, overwhelmed. "You'd do that?"

"For you? For us? Yes. I'd do anything."

"You don't have to."

"I do because I love you."

For a second she thought that maybe the crash of the ocean had distorted his words.

He framed her face with his hands and said it again. "I love you, Gillian Mitchell. After Dylan died I realized I'd never told him I loved him. We were thirteen and it just wasn't the sort of thing we'd say to each other. But it seemed so wrong and I felt so guilty about it and about being alive that since that day I've never said those words to anyone else I love, either. But, Gillian, you fill the places in me that Dylan's death left barren. Fill them so much that it hurts. In the best possible way. Like learning to use a limb that's been broken. I love Ethan and I love you. I love you together, I love you separately.

I want to marry you again—properly. I want to declare my love for you in a church with family and friends as witnesses to the fact that I'm going to share my life with you forever and always. I just need to hear you say those three words you said earlier one more time."

She kissed him gently, sweetly and drew back just enough to whisper, "I love you," before he was kissing her back.

Epilogue

The first few notes from the organ silenced the guests in the brimming Beverly Hills church. Sunlight streamed through high stained-glass windows and heads swiveled as Gillian took her first steps up the long aisle, the short train of her white dress trailing behind her.

So many faces. So many friends.

In six short months her life had changed almost beyond recognition.

Her gaze took it all in. The cavernous church seemed to swell with happiness. Hers and that of the guests. Everyone was smiling. Laura, flanked by the rest of her family, was smiling broadest of all, though she was also dabbing at her eyes with a dainty, white handkerchief.

Gillian's arm was linked through her mother's. The woman who'd been both mother and father to her was giving her away. Her mother, usually cynical about men, adored Max.

A sound behind her caught her attention and Gillian glanced back. Lilly and Nicole in their white-satin flower-girl dresses had stopped to help Ethan, who'd dropped the cushion that held their carefully chosen rings. Fortunately, the rings had been secured with a stitch to protect against just such an event.

Lilly picked up the velvet cushion and Nicole took Ethan's hand as Gillian turned back for the front. They'd make it there. Ethan had the girls helping, and failing that the church was filled with friends who'd be only too happy to assist. She saw Mrs. McDonald out of the corner of her eye, poised and ready to swoop to Ethan's aid. The race to help could well turn into a melee.

They were here for them not just today, but for the rest of their lives.

She looked ahead and found her true north when her gaze locked with Max's, the face of the rest of her life, and couldn't believe such utter happiness had come her way.

She felt herself drawn toward him. He looked so serious, so intense, so…proud. Her heart swelled even further.

Max was working for the Cara Miller Foundation now, helping the charity achieve amazing results.

The scent of white rosebuds drifted from the bouquet she held in front of the almost unnoticeable swell of her stomach. Six more months and Ethan would have a little brother or sister. And Max was possibly even more excited about the prospect than she was. He was already talking about possible names and plans for the nursery in their new home.

Drawn to the blue eyes watching her so intensely—as though she was the only woman, the only person, in the world—Gillian stopped in front of Max. His gaze softened on her as he reached for her hand and interlaced his fingers with hers, holding her as though he'd never let her go.

* * * * *

*Travel back fourteen years to spring break,
and a young Rafe Cameron dreaming
big against all odds. Turn the page for an exclusive
short story by USA TODAY bestselling author
Catherine Mann. And look for the next installment
in* THE TAKEOVER *miniseries,*
BOUGHT: HIS TEMPORARY FIANCÉE
*by Yvonne Lindsay,
wherever Silhouette books are sold.*

Rafe & Sarah—Part 3

Vista del Mar, California—Fourteen years ago

Checking her watch out of the corner of her eye, Sarah held her notepad in her hand, waiting for the five customers at patio table seven to make up their minds. Jeez, it was nine forty-five, for crying out loud, nearly the end of her shift and she was stuck waiting for them to decide who ordered what of the umpteen specially made dishes she'd brought to their table.

And yeah, she was getting antsy to punch out so she could go home and turn in early. Tomorrow, she and Rafe both had the day off, which never, never happened. They'd been lucky to find any time together over the past month.

Valentine's Day hadn't gone according to plans. But she was glad Rafe hadn't wasted a lot of money splurging on an expensive restaurant. She worked with fancy foods galore at the Vista del Mar Beach and Tennis Club. Honest to goodness, she preferred the simpler pleasures of life. She would take Grandma Kat's grilled cheeseburgers on a picnic blanket over pan-seared sea bass in a ritzy hot spot any day of the week. And the burgers cost a lot less.

Rafe had been flat broke on Valentine's Day because he'd paid the electric bill for his dad. Not that Rafe had told her the reason. She'd learned later from his father when Bob had thanked Rafe in front of her. Rafe had been embarrassed.

Sarah had been touched.

What an amazing guy she had, someone who would help his father out that way. So many boys at school expected money and cars just to be given to them without putting forth any effort. She saw too many overprivileged teenagers at work as well.

Like tonight.

Teenage vacationers on spring break were *the* worst. They thought it was their right to order her around because their daddies gave them flashy gold cards. Well, some things in life couldn't be bought at any price.

She hoped that message was getting through to Rafe, so he would quit trying to spend so much money on her. Honestly, she just wanted more time with him. And she would get that as soon as she finished her darn shift at table seven.

The current jerk in question pointed to his plate of prime rib with juice as red as his sunburned face. "This isn't what I ordered. I wanted the pan-seared sea bass."

She looked down at her order pad and saw clearly written prime rib. In fact, nobody at the table had even mentioned the sea bass until now. Hadn't mentioned it until they saw Mr. Worth at the table next to them get his when he came in from working late.

Mr. Worth always got the five-star treatment since he owned the town. But hey, it was her job to serve, much easier when the diner was someone like Mr. Worth who was always polite, even if he was stuffy.

"I'll swap this out for the sea bass right away." She scooped up the plate in front of the deep-fried spring breaker decked from head to toe in J. Crew and entitlement.

Arguing wouldn't get her anywhere anyway, and could likely bring a complaint she didn't need, especially when she was still so new to the payroll here.

The griping customer clamped his fingers around her wrist, his gold class ring broadcasting a highbrow prep school that had apparently failed to teach him manners. "You know, I've changed my mind. I'm not in the mood for sea bass after all."

"Okay, then…" She held her temper in check. "Is there something else you would like instead?"

"Call me Chip." He looked her up and down lewdly.

Sheesh, did he really think that was a turn-on?

Chip elbowed his friend beside him with a laugh and a wink before turning back to her. "What I want isn't on the menu, gorgeous."

He reached to grab her arm again.

She sidestepped quickly. "I'll ask the chef to come out and speak with you personally about his recommendations."

Sarah pivoted away, plate clutched in her white-knuckled fists. Someone pinched her thigh. Hard.

Ouch! She spun around, anger stinging to the roots of her red hair. Chip was grinning while his friends laughed.

Her face burned with embarrassment—and fury. She set down the prime rib on the table and reached for a pitcher of ice water, ready to upend it on to his sunburned head—

Quentin Dobbs, the usually quiet busboy, jostled her out of the way, dropping a tub of dishes. Mashed potatoes with asparagus splashed all over Chip's leather boat shoes.

Chip shot to his feet, jostling the table and flipping his

prime rib. "What the hell, dude? You wrecked my shoes and my dinner."

Shocked gasps from the customers filled the patio. Other diners stood to get out of the way of the drip, drip, drip of spilled water glasses sending rivulets down the linen tablecloth and on to the floor. Sarah set down the pitcher, looking over quickly at Mr. Worth's table, worried about this scene taking place in front of him. He simply shuffled his chair away from the pooling water and continued eating his own pan-seared sea bass, regally ignoring the chaos two feet away.

"Sorry about the mess." Quentin stepped in front of Sarah. "You weren't going to eat the prime rib anyway, right?"

Chip puffed out his beefy chest and crowded Quentin. "You are so fired."

"Someone made you the boss while I wasn't lookin'?" Quentin looked around, sweeping back his hair from his forehead as if it might have obstructed his view. "I could have sworn you needed a high school diploma for that job."

Sarah didn't know whether to wince or cheer as things escalated. But once the real manager walked over, it was all about the wincing as he ordered both Sarah and Quentin into the kitchen while he handled the matter himself.

A half hour later, Sarah hung up her apron in her locker and took out her purse. Her shift was over after a solid chewing out from the manager. At least she still had her job, unlike Quentin, who'd gotten fired.

Still irate, she walked out into the parking lot to her mom's "new" used car, a blue Toyota. While she was glad her parents had been able to afford a second vehicle after her mother's old one bit the dust, she missed having Rafe pick her up. Which was really kinda selfish since it meant his days were even longer. He already worked construction after school.

A shadow shifted against her car.

Her stomach took a roller-coaster dip, all thoughts of work

scattering. Rafe had come to see her after all. Her feet picked up the pace.

Only to slow.

The person lounging against her Toyota was shorter than Rafe and more muscular than lanky—waiting in the dark corner of the parking lot, ocean waves crashing against the bluff like in some freaky slasher movie. Her nerves gurgled.

She looked over her shoulder fast at the nearly deserted employees' lot. She pulled out her keychain with the mace on it, a gift from Rafe. He had been on her case about being safe and she should have listened. She backed away. The guy straightened, and she sagged with relief as recognition dawned.

"Quentin." She took in his familiar face and the same brown curls she'd once cut a chunk out of when she sat behind him in kindergarten, curious to test out her fancy new first-day-of-school scissors. "Oh. My. God. You scared me."

"I just wanted to be sure you made it to your car without any trouble from those guys."

"You sound like Rafe."

He clapped a hand over his chest. "After what I did for you tonight, you insult me that way? I'm wounded." He thumped his chest again. "Truly wounded."

Quentin was kind of funny when he wanted to be. "I know you two don't like each other, but he would say thanks if he was here." And she owed him a thanks and apology as well. "I'm sorry you lost your job because of me."

"Now hold on." He took her keys from her hand. "I lost my job because of those creeps, not you. So don't blame yourself. Besides, I don't really need the money and now I can enjoy the rest of my spring break."

Quentin's family wasn't rich, but they weren't hurting for money, either. His dad was the night shift manager at Worth

Industries. Quentin even had a pretty nice car of his own. Although…

"That still doesn't make it fair for you to lose your job over my problem."

"It's done. Now be careful, okay?" He opened her door for her. "Most teenage guys are bozos thinking with their, uh, hormones."

Laughing, she looked up at him as she slid into her car. "You're a teenage guy."

"Right." He patted the top of her car. "Good night, Sarah."

Rafe hefted himself up the sprawling oak tree beside Sarah's house. She slept in a second-floor room, the bedroom over the garage. Her parents were deep sleepers. Good thing. He was working twelve-hour days at the construction site to sock away some money during spring break. Tomorrow was supposed to be his day off, but they'd called him in to work an extra shift. And they were gonna pay *overtime*. That, he could not pass up.

Meanwhile, he had to do some fast talking to smooth this over with Sarah.

Potato bugs—or Jerusalem crickets as his dad called them— chirped in the quiet night. There weren't any car sounds that he could detect, and he was definitely listening hard. Swiping aside a low sweeping branch, he steadied himself on the tree limb and tapped on the glass pane. Shadows shifted inside the dimly lit room as Sarah came closer.

She cranked open the window and looked outside, checking past him quickly while grabbing his jacket to haul him inside. "You're crazy. I couldn't believe you were serious when you called to tell me to be on the lookout for you—and by the way, my dad was pissed when the phone rang so late on his night off."

"Sorry," he said simply, rolling to his feet and looking around her room for the first time.

Wow, he was really in here. Damn. It had been far too easy, and he was almost glad he hadn't thought of it sooner or he might have been way too tempted to see her on the sly when he had free moments at night.

Her walls were yellow, with posters of rock stars all over them. Bright like her. And on her bedside table rested a half-dead lily he'd given her a week ago…. Which reminded him.

Rafe pulled the rosebud from where he'd stuffed it inside his jacket to climb the tree. Helping out at the Worth estate greenhouse before school kept him well-stocked in flowers for Sarah, the one luxury he'd been able to give her.

Sarah took the flower and skimmed the petals under her nose, her smile huge. Then she was kissing him. The best part about giving her flowers. She leaned into him, her legs bare in her blue school gym shorts. And even through his jean jacket, he could tell she didn't have a bra on under her faded tank top. His hands shook as he tunneled them into her hair. Her hair was even softer than the flower.

Sighing, she eased back, her arms still looped around his neck. "How was work?"

"Long. Sweaty. How about you?"

"Busy. Lots of spring breakers." She looked away quickly. "After you called, I ran down to the kitchen and got you something to eat."

He looked past her to the blanket on her floor, set up like a picnic with a cheeseburger, chips and lemonade. Thank God. He was always starving these days, never enough time to grab more than a snack. Since his mom died three years ago, he and his dad hadn't cooked much. And now that his dad was going out with Penny, he'd pretty much stopped cooking altogether.

Rafe shrugged out of his jacket and dropped to the floor, leaning back against the wall. The cheeseburger was half gone before he realized he wasn't even talking. How lame that he was focused on stuffing his face when he was in the middle of Sarah's bedroom. She sat three feet away in a tank top and tiny gym shorts, leaning against the foot of her bed.

Her bed.

Another hunger shouted a great big hello inside him, urging him to toss back that yellow-and-green-striped bedspread and lay her down in the middle of the double mattress.

His body pulled tight, and he tossed the napkin over his lap while reaching for a handful of chips. "I should be taking you out." He downed the chips and another bite of the burger. "I still owe you a meal at Jacques's after the way I had to cancel on you at the last minute."

"Valentine's Day was wonderful because I was with you." She sipped from her own glass of lemonade. "We ate at the beach. We danced under the stars. It was perfect."

"You're perfect." He angled forward to climb past the food, toward her.

She nudged his shoulder, pushing him back down to sit. "Nope. Finish your supper, and maybe you can even talk a little."

"Talk about what?" He finished off the cheeseburger. The faster he ate, apparently the sooner he would get to make out with Sarah.

"You never did tell me how you managed such a good meal for the Valentine's picnic. I know for a fact that you and your dad can't cook worth a darn."

"Dad's friend Penny helped."

Sometimes Penny even left food in the kitchen. She'd found him standing in front of the pathetically empty refrigerator and offered to help. She'd shared the picnic dinner she'd made for his dad on Valentine's Day.

Getting used to his father dating someone else was tougher than he'd expected. Getting over his mother's death was even tougher. But his dad really liked Penny and there wasn't a thing Rafe could do about that.

Best to focus on what he could change. He moved a half-finished history class collage and brushed aside stray cut-out articles from the *Seaside Gazette*. "We're wasting time, and we don't get nearly enough together."

"I agree." She rose up on to her knees and reached for him.

Moving fast, he scooped her into his arms, eyeing her nice soft bed, conveniently located two steps away. When he turned, she wriggled against his chest, her breasts so soft and perfect against him.

"Careful," he teased. "Wouldn't want to drop you and wake up the whole house."

Jokingly, he tossed her lightly, confident there wasn't a chance in hell he would ever drop her. He caught her smoothly.

She gasped, wincing.

He frowned. "What's wrong?"

"Nothing," she said quickly, too quickly.

He set her on her feet again and looked her over in front, then in back. A quarter-size, fresh bruise was purpling up on her thigh.

"What happened to your leg?"

She twisted to look at the back of her thigh, then shrugged. "Oh, um, I must have, well, bumped against a table at work, I mean backed up into something."

Her stumbling explanation sent his instincts on alert. "You're a really bad liar."

"Fine…" She rolled her eyes dismissively. "Some spring breaker at the restaurant got fresh."

Rage exploded behind his eyes hot and fast. "Who?" he demanded. "I want his name."

Sarah rested a hand on his chest, smoothing his T-shirt. "He's probably already left town."

"Doesn't matter." Five minutes. He only needed five minutes to pry an apology for Sarah from the jerk's mouth.

"No," she said, as if reading his mind. "You're not going to get rich if you're in jail for kicking some moron's butt."

"That's assuming I would get caught. Who is he?"

"Believe me, he's already sorry." She crinkled her nose, grinning. "Quentin dumped an order of mashed potatoes on the guy's expensive shoes."

His anger cooled to something else entirely. "Quentin Dobbs protected you?"

"I could have taken care of myself. And believe me, I would have and it would have cost me my job." She sat on the edge of the bed, clasping his hands in hers lightly while he stood stock still. "Quentin did more than take care of the problem. He kept me from doing something rash. I know you don't like him, but for tonight, he's the good guy. He's on our side, okay?"

He bit back the words he wanted to say. Bottom line, he owed Quentin. As much as that stung, Rafe always paid his debts. He refused to owe anyone. Ever.

That didn't mean he would let Dobbs suffer any delusions about who Sarah belonged with. Because come graduation, Sarah would be leaving town with him.

An hour later, Sarah grabbed Rafe's wrist and pulled his hand out from under her tank top.

"Enough," she gasped, flopping onto her back on her bed. Her comforter had long ago been kicked to the floor as they rolled around making out. "If we keep going, I'm not sure if I can stop, and I'm just not ready. Okay?"

Breathing heavy, he rolled onto his side, toying with her hair, his eyes lingering on her chest. Where he'd been touching her two seconds ago. Driving her absolutely crazy. She pressed her legs together against the ache that built more and more every time she was with Rafe.

"Okay, Sarah, we're both eighteen, adults, but it's your call." He still played with a lock of her hair, but otherwise kept his hands to himself.

She knew that had to be costing him. She'd felt just how bad he wanted her. "We'll have to make sure we're at a really public beach tomorrow so we don't get too tempted."

His eyes slid away from hers again, this time scanning the rock posters on her wall. "Someday, I'm going to give you a real vacation. I'll take you to the best concerts in the biggest cities. How about London?"

"I'm happy with a day at the beach. And who wants to waste all our time together traveling? What's wrong with a simple drive to San Diego?"

"I offer you England and you want somewhere we've seen before?" He tugged her hair lightly. "Where's your sense of adventure?"

She nudged his bare foot with hers. "You're about as much adventure as I can take."

"Okay, let's try this again. If you could plan a vacation anywhere—" He rushed to add, "Anywhere other than California, where would it be?"

She thought hard. That kind of life seemed so far in the future, but if playing the what-if game would make Rafe happy, then okay. "I would want someplace where we could be alone, just the two of us. No interruptions."

Totally committed. Totally married. But she kept that part of the dream to herself for now.

Thank God he hadn't seen the inside of her history notebook when he'd shuffled her project around, since she'd practiced writing Mrs. Rafe Cameron about a hundred and fifty times during class.

He tucked her closer. "Alone together sounds good. Continue."

Snuggling against his side, she listened to his heartbeat and inhaled the clean soapy scent on his neck. "No work or obligations. But it would still need to feel homey. I wouldn't want some generic hotel room."

"So you want to own a vacation home." His knuckles skimmed along her back, up and down her spine deliciously. "Where would you like to build it?"

"A *vacation* home?" She wouldn't have to move, and she wouldn't be stuck in some stark hotel. "Yes, I guess that would work."

"Everything would be there for you so you wouldn't even need to pack. Now, where?" he asked again.

"If a person's going to have a vacation house, then it should be somewhere different than where you live every day. I can go to the beach anytime. Somewhere cooler maybe." She blew against his neck lightly. "The mountains, I think. A ski cabin with a pond."

"Keep going." He dug his head back into the pillow.

"Nevada." She plucked the state out of the sky at random, somewhere not too far away. "A woodsy, homey cabin that has high ceilings with big fat beams and windows that take up an entire wall."

"Consider it yours."

"You're so funny." She arched up to kiss his jaw. "Really though, I just want more time with you. And if you're working eighteen-hour days to buy us stuff, then what's the use? We won't get to enjoy them together."

He stayed quiet, their old money versus simple pleasures argument sort of bouncing around in the air between them like a beach ball just out of reach.

She hated wasting her time arguing with him, but she also wasn't the type to simply back down. She toed an itch on the bottom of her foot, thinking. Waiting. Hoping he would say something.

"Crap!" Rafe bolted upright. "Somebody's awake downstairs.

"Ohmigod!" She rolled to her knees quickly. Listening.

The bottom step creaked, just like it always did when someone started walking up. Rafe jumped off the bed, grabbed his jacket and shoes while Sarah shoved their picnic under her bed. He raced for the window, checking outside quickly before swinging a leg out.

Sarah clasped his hand, stopping him. "I'm sorry," she whispered fast. "I hate to fight. I'll make it up to you tomorrow. We'll have a great day hanging out by the ocean. You'll see."

"About the beach." He hesitated, half in, half out of the window. "I'll call you in the morning."

"Okay, okay, hurry. You need to go before my mom or dad finds you, or we'll never get to see each other again."

Rafe cupped the back of her head and kissed her hard, fast. "Nevada cabin. I won't forget."

Her toes curling into the carpet, she watched him climb down the tree like it was nothing. He managed everything that way. She could almost believe he might build that Nevada cabin someday.

The footsteps creaked just outside her door.

Spinning fast, she yanked the rumpled bedspread off the floor and dove under her covers. Tucking the extra pillow to her chest, she closed her eyes just as her mom peeked in to check on her then closed the door softly again.

With the light scent of the rose still hanging in the air,

Sarah thought about the way Rafe had asked what she wanted for a vacation. She started to hope he was finally seeing things her way about a simpler life together.

* * * * *

Silhouette® Desire

COMING NEXT MONTH

Available April 12, 2011

REQUEST YOUR FREE BOOKS!

2 FREE NOVELS PLUS 2 FREE GIFTS!

Silhouette® Desire®

Passionate, Powerful, Provocative!

SDES11

Selene wanted nothing to do with the father of her son, Alex; but Aristedes had other plans...that included them.

Read on for an sneak peek from
THE SARANTOS SECRET BABY by Olivia Gates,
available April 2011, only from Harlequin Desire.

"You were right to turn my marriage offer down," Aristedes said.

And Selene found her voice at last, found the words that would not betray the blow he'd dealt her. "Thanks for letting me know. You didn't have to come all the way here, though. You could have just let it go. I left yesterday with the understanding that this case is closed."

Before the hot needles behind her eyes could dissolve into an unforgivable display of stupidity and weakness, she began to close the door.

The door stopped against an immovable object. His flat palm.

"I can't accept that." His voice was low, leashed.

What did her tormentor mean now? Was he ending one game only to start another?

She raised eyes as bruised as her self-respect to his, found nothing there but solemnity and determination.

Before she could voice her confusion, he elaborated. "I never let anything go unless I'm certain it's unworkable. I realize I made you an unworkable offer, and that's why I'm withdrawing it. I'm here to offer something else. A workability study."

She leaned against the door, thankful for its support and partial shield. "Your son and I are not a business venture you can test for feasibility."

His gaze grew deeper, made her feel as if he was trying to delve into her mind, take control of it. "It's actually the other way around. I'm the one who would be tested."

She shook her head. "Why bother? I know—and *you* know—you're not workable. Not with me."

His spectacular eyebrows lowered over eyes she felt were emitting silver hypnosis. "You're right again. Neither you nor I have any reason to believe that isn't the truth. The only truth. It might be best for both you and Alex to never hear from me again, to forget I exist. But then again, maybe not. I'm only asking for the chance for both of us to find out for certain. You believe I'm unworkable in any personal relationship. I've lived my life based on that belief about myself. I never really had reason to question it. But I have one now. In fact, I have two."

Find out what happens in
THE SARANTOS SECRET BABY by Olivia Gates,
available April 2011, only from Harlequin Desire.

Harlequin *Blaze*™
red-hot reads

Sunny, sensual Hawaiian spring break…again!

Three best girlfriends are recapturing an amazing spring-break
vacation they had a decade ago.

First on the beach is former attorney and all-around good girl
Mia Butterfield. Meeting up with her boyfriend of old is a bust,
so she's shocked when her hero turns out to be someone she'd
never have expected…

Find out who it is in
SECOND TIME LUCKY
by acclaimed author
Debbi Rawlins

Available from Harlequin Blaze® April 2011

Part of the sensual miniseries,
Spring Break
Part 2: Delicious Do-Over (May)

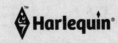

Harlequin®

A *Romance* FOR EVERY MOOD™

www.eHarlequin.com

HB79607

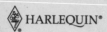